Also by Cynthia A. Graham

Beneath Still Waters
Behind Every Door

BETWEEN
THE
LIES

BETWEEN THE LIES

a Hick Blackburn Mystery

by

CYNTHIA A. GRAHAM

Blank Slate Press | Saint Louis, MO

Blank Slate Press
an imprint of Amphorae Publishing Group LLC
Saint Louis, MO 63116

A Hick Blackburn Book

For information, contact
Blank Slate Press at 4168 Hartford Street, Saint Louis, MO 63116
www.amphoraepublishing.com
Manufactured in the United States of America
Cover Design by Kristina Blank Makansi
Cover Art: Shutterstock / IStock

ISBN: 9781943075447

For Sandy Crane, the sister of my heart.
Gone, but not forgotten. Never forgotten.

I
Friday, July 16, 1954

Waves of heat danced above the asphalt as Sheriff Hick Blackburn turned onto the highway and headed out of Cherokee Crossing. The call from Father Jefferson Davis Grant, pastor of the small Catholic Church in Broken Creek, had been a surprise, and Hick's decision to pay the priest a visit hadn't set well with Adam. As both Hick's deputy and his brother-in-law, Adam Kinion was the older, and sometimes wiser, friend Hick relied on for advice. And in this case, Hick thought, Adam was probably right. Hick knew he probably couldn't be much help with whatever problem Father Grant was facing in Broken Creek, a town located clear over in another county and run by a sheriff that didn't look kindly on outside interference in local affairs. Adam had been against the visit, but it seemed wrong to ignore the man's request for help. "Help with what?" Adam had asked. Hick had no idea, but figured he ought to at least find out.

"I'm just going to talk to him and see what's on his mind," Hick said as he picked up his hat.

Adam plopped his feet up on the desk and settled in for the night shift. "You're wasting your time. Why would he call you, anyway?"

"That's what I'm gonna find out."

It had been four years since Hick and Father Grant had discussed the governor's refusal to posthumously exonerate Abner Delaney, a man unjustly executed for the murder of a young woman in Cherokee Crossing, and since then they had neither seen nor spoken to each other. *Why now?* Hick wondered. By the time he pulled into the parking lot, the late-evening sun was sinking toward the horizon, painting the sky gold and pink on its way. Behind the church, struggling cotton plants spread out in neat rows giving the scene a timeless feel, as if Our Lady of Sorrows was stuck in the kind of painting that used to hang along the hallways of the Cherokee Crossing High School.

It hadn't rained in weeks and the lot was dusty and rutted. On the porch, wilting red geraniums stood in cracked, flaking flower pots. Hick climbed the crooked steps, hesitated and then pulled the door open and stepped inside. The office was just as he remembered—the same pictures on the wall, the same shabby neatness. But the desk of Miss Esther Burton was empty and Father Grant's office door was open. Hick removed his hat and started toward the office when the priest appeared in the doorway. Four years had done little to change the man, other than sprinkle more gray in his beard. He was still an imposing presence, tall, with dark, intense eyes.

"I wasn't sure you'd really come," the priest said, extending his hand.

Hick shrugged. "Like I said on the phone, I doubt there's much I can do."

Without another word, Father Grant disappeared into the office, leaving Hick to follow. At the threshold, Hick paused. The young secretary, Esther Burton, was in a chair, weeping quietly into a handkerchief. The office was not as chaotic as Hick remembered, though no one would call it neat. The *What Is Man That Thou Art Mindful Of Him?* sampler had been replaced with one that read, *For he that loveth not his brother, whom he seeth, how can he love God, whom he seeth not?* The amber colored decanters were no longer on the credenza, but the radio still played softly in the corner. On the desk lay a newspaper.

"Sit. Please." Grant waved at a chair. "You remember my secretary, Esther?"

Nodding, Hick sat and glanced at Esther who studied him as she dabbed her eyes. "What's this all about?"

The priest sat behind his desk and handed Hick a newspaper. "Negro Runs Down Vagrant," the headline read. Hick looked from Esther to Grant then put the newspaper back on the desk.

Grant tapped the paper. "Something's not right about this."

"Go on," Hick said.

"The young man accused is Thaddeus Burton." Grant cocked his head toward the young woman. "Esther's little brother."

"And?"

"We don't think he did it." Grant paused and then added, "In fact, we know he didn't do it."

Hick had seen this kind of denial before. It was the same when Claire Thompson had been arrested six years ago for the murder of an infant. It was the same when Elizabeth Shelley had been arrested. It was always hard for folks to understand that the heart of a killer could lurk beneath the kindest face.

Grant must have read the skepticism in Hick's eyes because he added, "He's only twelve years old."

Twelve. The same age as Hick's nephew, Henry. Hick picked up the paper and scanned the report. It stated that the accused, Thaddeus Burton, had stolen a truck and that, unable to see over the steering wheel, had negligently hit an unidentified vagrant and subsequently panicked, fleeing the scene. "Tell me why you think this is wrong."

"Sheriff, these kids get little to eat and hardly no meat." Grant kneaded his temple and then ran his hand through his hair. "He's small for his age. I don't think he's strong or tall enough to even push in the clutch."

Hick shrugged. "The story corroborates what you're saying about the young man's size."

Grant leaned toward Hick, a bitter smirk on his lips. "Thaddeus Burton wouldn't know how to start a truck or even put it in gear. I'm telling you something's wrong with this whole thing. They're saying he went to school on July 13, like every other Tuesday, and that in the night he slipped out of his house, got into this truck, somehow figured out how to drive the thing, and ran over a man miles away. Then, he was so 'panicked' he simply went home, climbed into bed, and fell into a deep sleep."

The summer session of school was a cotton belt peculiarity, a way to enable the kids, both black and white, to be out of school during cotton picking in October. Hick never worked the cotton fields, but he remembered how much he hated attending school in the heat of the summer when he could've been fishing.

Esther interrupted his memories of stifling school rooms. She stood and looked down at Hick. "Sheriff, our colored school is fourteen miles away. Thad has to be out the door by six o'clock of a morning." Her eyes held his. "That boy was sound asleep when I went to wake him up. He was clean, he hadn't been walking on no dirt roads or through no fields. He didn't have as much as one burr on his pants." Her lips trembled. "He was in his bed all night. I know it. Thad is a good boy. There ain't no way he'd a snuck out at night. He chattered away over his breakfast like every other day and then climbed on that bus without a care in the world."

Hick looked again at the newspaper. The unidentified man was killed on the outskirts of town sometime in the early hours of the morning on Wednesday. Even with an almost full moon it seemed highly unlikely that, in the state described, the young boy could walk all the way home, fall sound asleep, and behave completely normal the next day.

"Where's the truck now?" Hick asked.

Grant glanced at Esther, then looked back at Hick. "It's impounded at the station."

"And where's Thaddeus?"

"Also at the station."

Hick turned to Esther. "Has your brother been charged?"

"No," Esther said, her voice tight with anger—and fear.

"Brewster told the family that Thad has been brought in for 'safekeeping'," Grant said.

Hick frowned at the mention of Sheriff Earl Brewster, a man he regarded with contempt and one he'd prefer to avoid. The two men had a strained professional relationship since Brewster dismantled one of the first cases of Hick's career. The older man had taken great pleasure in pointing out the defects of a case against Mule and Hoyt Smith, two men with whom Brewster had a family connection

"The boy hasn't been charged, hasn't had a hearing," Grant continued, sarcasm lacing each word. "The judge and the prosecutor are both out of town on a fishing trip and won't be back until next Wednesday, so for a week he's expected to sit in that jail and wait."

Hick shook his head. "What about a lawyer?"

"I suppose he'll have an attorney appointed if it goes to trial."

Hick looked up. "What do you mean, 'if'?"

"Sheriff Brewster told my daddy that the best thing for Thad to do is to plead guilty," Esther said.

Hick's brows knitted together. "Why would he plead guilty if he's innocent?"

Grant leaned forward in his chair. "Sheriff Brewster has been riding the family hard to get a confession."

Hick picked up the newspaper and scanned the story one more time. "Why would Brewster think Thaddeus is involved in the first place? What would be the motive for taking the truck?"

"Thad chops cotton for Grover Sutton after school and it was Sutton's truck that ran over the man," Esther said. "He was sitting on the running board after work on Tuesday, and Mr. Sutton had to shoo him away."

"That's it?"

"Truthfully, Thad knew the keys were kept in the truck, but so did everyone else. It was common knowledge."

"And somehow, that's enough for Sutton to implicate Thad in the theft." Grant grimaced as if he had a bad taste in his mouth. "The only motive mentioned was a joy ride. As ludicrous as this whole thing is, that was all the proof our sheriff seemed to need to drag Thaddeus out of school first thing Wednesday morning in handcuffs."

In the paper, Hick had noted, the victim was struck by the vehicle and died instantly at the scene. "When was the truck reported missing?"

"Sheriff told my daddy that Sutton woke before dawn and noticed it was gone. Sutton called him and Sheriff went looking for it. Says he found the truck outside of town, in the ditch." She shuddered. "And that man's body was just lying on the road."

"The poor guy was hit with a half-ton pickup." Grant shook his head. "He didn't have a chance."

"What did Brewster say happened next?"

"He told the Burtons he'd called the coroner and they went over the scene," Grant said. "Then they took the body to the undertaker, and drove the truck to the station."

"Well, the truck is contaminated then. They can't use any prints from it as evidence."

"You're wrong," Esther shot back, her eyes flashing.

"If the police or coroner contaminated—" Hick started to explain.

"Sheriff Blackburn," Esther interrupted, "the first thing Brewster did after dragging my brother out of school was to have him sit in that truck to see if he could drive it. I was there. I watched. I assure you there are plenty of Thad's prints in that truck, and I won't be a bit surprised if Brewster finds a way to use them." She walked to the window and stared out. Hick could see her shoulders rise and fall as she sobbed quietly.

"That boy couldn't even push in the clutch," Grant said in a low, quiet voice. "We suspect Brewster put Thad in that truck to make sure the boy's prints were there."

Hick's eyes widened. "What are you saying?"

Father Grant rose and flipped off the radio. He turned to Hick and said, "I wish someone could explain to me how a boy could go home from work, get up in the middle of the night, go back to Sutton's place, steal a truck he can't drive, run over a man, abandon the truck, and have the presence of mind to walk home in the dark, go to bed, and simply get up the next morning, have breakfast, and go to school as if nothing ever happened." He paused. "The truck was found way out on County Road 14. Clear on the other side of town."

Hick tossed the newspaper back onto the desk. "So, no witnesses and no physical evidence to tie Thad to the scene, except for highly questionable fingerprints. There's the improbability of the timeline and questions about his physical ability to drive the truck. This all adds up, by definition, to reasonable doubt. The charge would be unlikely to stand in court. It simply doesn't make sense. No judge on earth would send this to trial."

"That may or may not be true, but the fact of the matter is Brewster will get Thad to plead. I've seen it before. Sheriff Brewster has worked hard to convince the family it's in Thad's best interest to say he's guilty. The fact that he's a minor weighs heavily. He'll only go to the juvenile farm until he's eighteen. Brewster's already told the family that if they fight the charges Thad could be charged with vehicular manslaughter as an adult, and Brewster can be very convincing. You know as well as I do how the system works for Negroes."

Hick exhaled, his arguments deflated in an instant. "Why would he accuse the boy if it's so obvious he couldn't have done this?"

Father Grant returned to his chair. "Someone killed a man with that truck, but I guarantee Brewster doesn't believe for a minute it was Thad Burton. Perhaps it's as simple as the fact that Thad's a convenient scapegoat. That would not be unusual here in Broken Creek."

"So you think Brewster doesn't want to put in the effort?"

Leaning forward, Father Grant held Hick's gaze. "Unfortunately, I think it's worse than that. I think Brewster might actually know who did this."

Hick stared. "You accusing Brewster of a cover-up?"

Grant glanced at Esther who had turned her back on the window and was watching the two men. "Sheriff, I know, as do you, that Brewster is as corrupt as the day is long. I have watched him arrest colored folk time after time with little or no evidence, and I have seen judges sentence them for crimes they did not commit." A muscle along Grant's jaw clenched. "Brewster and I are not friends. He knows I know what he does, but he also knows there's nothing I can do about it. He lords that over me every chance he gets. You recall that as a Catholic I'm an outsider in this town, and Brewster's been clear from the day I arrived that I'm not welcome."

"Have you talked to the boy?"

"I've been to the jailhouse several times, but they won't let me near him."

Hick knew what the family was up against and that there was little he could do to help. Still, he couldn't just walk away. He turned to Esther. "You know they don't have to talk with me either and probably won't. I can make a professional call and see that your brother is being treated well." He glanced at Grant. "Will that ease your minds?"

Esther's eyes were red-rimmed from crying and the look she gave Hick told him his gesture was appreciated, but that it clearly wasn't enough.

"There's a young deputy by the name of Royal Adkins who just hired on with Brewster," Grant said, drawing Hick's attention back from Esther. "He knows the Burton family well. Hopefully, Brewster hasn't had enough time to corrupt him. Maybe he'll help us."

Hick looked at Father Grant in surprise. "Help *us*?"

"I can't do this alone. I need you."

2

Friday, July 16, 1954

Hick turned off the car, blew out a trail of cigarette smoke, and stared at the building across the street. The Broken Creek Sheriff's office was a carbon copy of the office he occupied in Cherokee Crossing, but this place seemed dingier, like a penny that had lost its shine. The last rays of the setting sun glinted on the front windows and reflected back a harsh glow, almost as if the place was on fire within. Maybe it was. Maybe the whole world was on fire and always would be. He ran a hand down his face and scoffed at his philosophical frame of mind. Yet he knew that corrupt lawmen were dangerous and Sheriff Earl Brewster, who had operated largely at will for years, was more dangerous than most. It was tempting to put the car in gear and drive straight back to Cherokee Crossing. But then he thought of Henry. And Thaddeus Burton sitting inside. Alone. Only twelve years old.

Sighing, Hick tossed the cigarette out the window and pulled his hat down over his eyes, ready for the battle ahead.

He pulled the door open and relief flooded through him as he quickly noted that Sheriff Brewster was not in the office.

The young deputy looked up and smiled. "Howdy. I'm Deputy Royal Adkins. What can I do for you?"

"Just passing through," Hick said pleasantly. "Thought I'd pay a call on Sheriff Brewster and see how he's doing. He in?"

"No, Sheriff," the deputy answered after a quick glance at Hick's badge. "He's gone home for the day. You want me to try and call him back?"

"No need for that. I expect I'll catch up with him another time." Hick was only twenty-eight and the deputy looked even younger. Adkins had dark, unruly hair, a long, straight nose, and a thin face. Hick looked around the office until his gaze fell on the cell in the back of the building. In it a small black boy stared despondently at his bare feet. His hair was cropped close to his head, most likely to keep him cool as he worked the fields, and he was wearing denim overalls and a white T-shirt from which emerged thin, but muscular arms. He didn't look to be as tall as Henry and most considered Henry short for his age. The boy seemed to be physically cared for, but Hick could sense his fear clear across the room.

Hick nodded toward the cell. "What have you got there?"

The young deputy rose, reached into his shirt pocket, and pulled out a pack of chewing gum. Putting a stick of Beech-Nut into his mouth, he said, "This is Thaddeus Burton. Thad's a good kid, but I reckon we all make mistakes. Sheriff Brewster says he killed a man outside of town."

"He's awful small," Hick replied. "How'd he do it?"

"Hit him with a truck."

"A truck? Looks like he's hardly big enough to work the clutch."

The young deputy said nothing as Hick walked over to the cell. "Your people got a truck?" Hick asked Thad.

Without looking up, Thad shook his head.

"He snuck out in the middle of the night and borrowed a truck from Grover Sutton," the deputy said. "Sutton's the farmer he chops cotton for."

"I didn't take no truck," Thaddeus mumbled to no one in particular.

"You know how to drive?" Hick asked.

Thaddeus raised his eyes to Hick's face. "No, sir. I ain't never drove no car."

"Now, Thad," Deputy Adkins said, "we done been through this. Sheriff Brewster says you're right smart. Ain't nothing at all for a smart kid like you to figure it out."

Thad shook his head and stared again at his feet.

Hick glanced out the window at the large pick-up truck beside the station. "That the truck?"

"One and the same."

"I reckon that thing bucked and jumped like a son of a bitch."

Thad looked at him uncomprehendingly and Deputy Adkins asked, "What do you mean?"

"I just remember my daddy teaching me to drive and how hard it was to let the clutch up just right. I reckon that truck must have a real easy clutch if this boy could figure out how to put her in gear all by himself."

Royal scratched his head. "Well, now you mention it, Sutton's always complaining about the clutch being finicky."

"Seems a might strange a boy could teach himself to drive so well in such a short time that he figured out how to get around, in the middle of the night, in the dark, when he can barely see out the windshield."

Royal rubbed his hand along the back of his neck and let out a soft whistle. "Don't know about all that. Sheriff Brewster says he done it, that's all I know."

"You even know what a clutch is used for, Thaddeus?" Hick asked, turning to the young boy.

Thad looked up at Hick and shook his head.

"You know what them pedals on the floor are for?"

"I reckon one makes it go and one makes it stop."

"What about the third one?"

"What you need a third for?" Thad asked.

Royal frowned and turned to Hick. "You don't think he did it?"

Hick pulled out a cigarette. "I don't know. This is the first I've met Thaddeus, but you've got to admit it's a little hard to swallow." He let that hang in the air for a moment as he lit his cigarette and took a drag. "Like I said, I'm just paying a call. I'll be on my way now."

"What'd you say your name was?"

"Blackburn," Hick replied. "Sheriff Hick Blackburn from Cherokee Crossing."

Royal went back to his desk and wrote the name down. "I'll be sure and tell Sheriff Brewster you come to call and was making some good points."

"Do that," Hick answered and stepped outside. He paused on the porch and watched the red sun sinking behind the distant tree line. If he wanted to look over the truck, he'd have to hurry.

A quick glance at the vehicle confirmed that Brewster had gotten at least part of his investigation right. The truck had obviously been in a collision with a pedestrian, but now that Hick had met Thaddeus Burton, he knew there was no way he'd been the one driving. He paused before climbing into his car and glanced again at the Broken Creek station. The sunlight's harsh reflection on the windows had been replaced by the soft glow of a desk lamp shining inside. He had planted a seed of doubt in Deputy Royal Adkin's mind, of that Hick was sure. Now to wait and see what would come of it.

3
Friday, July 16, 1954

Lights shone through the back windows of the house and illuminated the yard as Hick pulled into Dr. Jacob Prescott's driveway. Jake had always been a fixture in Hick's world. He had been his father's best friend and for many years, Hick's confidante. Jake was someone who seemed to have the answers Hick needed. And he needed answers—and guidance—now.

After looking over the damage to the truck, Hick had driven out through Broken Creek and down County Road 14 until he found the crime scene. The headlights of his squad car had shown clearly where the man lost his life, the blood-stains on the ground, the tire marks in the gravel. He understood the physical evidence on the truck and at the scene, but he hoped Jake could help him understand what was going on inside the mind of the perpetrator.

A haloed moon shone down through the cool, humid darkness and the chirping of crickets filled the air. Hick climbed the steps, opened the screen door, and knocked, stepping back to avoid the moths banging against the porch light. As Jake aged, he seemed to sleep less and lately it had become common to see light spilling out at all hours. The sound of footsteps moved closer to the door and Jake's face appeared on the other side. "Everything okay?" he asked, stepping back and letting Hick inside.

Hick entered the dark front entry room and removed his hat. "Everything's fine. I saw your light and knew you were awake. Just wondering if you have a minute. I have a couple of questions."

"Sure," Jake said, leading Hick to the back of the house and into the study where he had evidently been reading. He put the book aside and picked up a glass, taking a drink of his regular evening tumbler of bourbon. "Can I get you anything?"

"No, thanks," Hick said, sitting in a leather armchair and lighting a cigarette.

"Is Maggie feeling okay?"

"Mag's fine. She's convinced this baby will be a girl," Hick said, remembering the certainty with which his wife had made the declaration.

Jake smiled and sat back, running a cigar beneath his nose before lighting it. "Women often have a sense about these things." He puffed his cigar and studied his young friend. "So, tell me what's on your mind."

Hick took a long drag of his cigarette then tapped his ashes in the nearby ashtray. "What do you know about panic?"

Jake eyed him. "Panic? Why do you ask?"

"A man was killed over in Broken Creek—run over by a half-ton truck. Brewster nabbed a twelve-year-old kid but there are a few things that just don't add up."

"Like?"

"They say this boy, probably not even as tall as Henry, panicked after he hit the man. The newspaper report said he wasn't thinking straight and that's why he didn't report the accident."

"That makes sense. I'm sure he was frightened beyond reason."

"But tell me," Hick said leaning forward, "would a kid, supposedly 'frightened beyond reason' have the presence of mind to walk home and fall into a deep sleep? If he was panicked would he simply have breakfast as usual, climb on the bus as usual, and go to school the next morning like all was right with the world?"

"The little I know of panic makes me think he would not. It's a fight or flight instinct. His adrenaline would be pumping. I doubt he could stop his heart from pounding and his mind from racing. Do we know he was asleep at home? Maybe he was tossing and turning, frightened he would be caught."

Hick stabbed his cigarette out. "Yeah, maybe."

"You don't think he did it?"

"Not for a second. He's so small and that truck is huge and hard to drive. Owner himself had complained that the clutch was finicky and the kid didn't even know what a clutch is. Thought all you needed was a pedal to go and a pedal to stop."

"Well, what about injuries to the child?"

"What?"

"How fast was he going?"

"Judging from the skid marks on the gravel, pretty damn fast."

"Well, if he's as small as you say, at the very least he would have sustained some sort of facial laceration upon impact."

Hick shook his head. "I saw him. He didn't have as much as a hangnail." He paused and stared into the distance, picturing Thaddeus Burton sitting behind the wheel of the truck. "You're pretty certain the driver would be injured?"

"Yes," Jake replied. "The driver would certainly have sustained some sort of injury upon impact. They could have facial bruising from hitting the steering wheel or being thrown into the windshield, and wrist, knee, or ankle injuries, even broken ribs." Jake took a long sip of bourbon. "But this happened in Broken Creek, not Cherokee Crossing."

"That priest asked me to look into it. The one that tried to help Abner Delaney."

Jake took another sip and stared over his glass at Hick. "But what can you do?"

"I don't know. Maybe nothing." Hick stood to leave.

"Before you go ..." Jake moved to his desk, picked up a pill bottle, and held it out to Hick.

"What's this?"

"Water pills for Maggie. She's not due for another appointment for a while, but I saw her in town and she's awful swollen." Jake took his handkerchief and wiped his neck. "It's probably this blistering heat."

"Thanks Doc." Hick held the bottle up to read the label. "I'll see she gets these."

"Give her my best, and tell her to take care of herself," Jake said, as Hick stepped out onto the porch. "Doctor's orders."

Hick said goodbye, climbed into the car, and lit another cigarette. He took a drag, and put the car into gear. Thad Burton might be completely uninjured, he thought, but someone in Broken Creek was not.

∽

He turned off the headlights before pulling into the driveway and opened the door as quietly as possible. Inside, he sat the car keys on the kitchen table beside a note that read, "Dinner's in icebox. Wake me when you get home. Love, Mag." He crossed the room and grabbed a chicken leg from the icebox, then crept to the door of his sons' room and peered inside. The kitchen light slanted into the room revealing two little boys. Jimmy rested peacefully, but the youngest, Jake, named for the doctor, mumbled something in his sleep, his arms flung wide open, one leg over the side of the bed, his dark hair contrasting against the white pillowcase. They both lay outside the sheets, trying to stay cool in the July heat that bore down on the house even at night.

Hick closed their door and tossed the chicken bone into the trash before entering his own room, carefully avoiding the boards he knew would creak. He had just taken off his shoes when Maggie rolled over. "What time is it?"

"It's late." He hung his pants over a chair. "Go back to sleep."

"Did you eat?"

"Yeah."

She pushed herself up into a sitting position and plumped the pillow behind her. "Well, where have you been?"

Hick draped his shirt over the chair back and crept across the room. "Just needed to give someone some professional advice. We can talk about it tomorrow."

"I'd rather talk about it now."

"I'll be here in the morning. Can't we talk then?" Even as he said it, he regretted it. He sat on the bed knowing full well it was his fault they had trouble communicating. And that his reluctance to share details about his work—and about his often-conflicted feelings about all sorts of things—only caused her to be even more persistent. Owning this responsibility did nothing to lessen his irritation.

"Why are you so late? What were you doing?"

"I had to see someone in another town. A friend just asked me if I'd take a look at a case."

"A friend? Why doesn't he talk to the local sheriff?"

Hick let out a reluctant sigh. "It's Brewster."

Maggie's eyes narrowed. "Earl Brewster?"

"Yeah."

"Hickory, whatever it is, you can't get involved in it. That man is crooked and dangerous." Hick figured she was thinking of Brewster's testimony at the Smith trial seven years earlier. Maggie understood enough about Brewster to realize he enjoyed making others look bad and would resent any interference. Especially from the young upstart, Hick Blackburn.

"I went over to see that Catholic preacher, the one that tried to help Abner Delaney."

Mourning Delaney, Abner's daughter, was like family. She had moved in with Hick and Maggie after her mother died four years earlier, and was completely devoted to Maggie. Maggie's love of Mourning and her respect for the man who had tried to help the girl's father softened her attitude. "What did he want with you?"

"Brewster's locked up Father Grant's secretary's little brother. The kid's Henry's age." He slid his legs under the sheet. "Just twelve-years-old."

"What on earth do they think he did?"

The light from a full moon streamed through the window and heightened the pallor of Maggie's once bronze skin. Her face was puffy and swollen. The last thing Hick wanted was for her to worry. Why wouldn't she let him stay in his own world and not demand to be part of it? Why did she want to trouble herself with details that would do her no good? He hesitated, but knew ignoring the question was not an option.

"They say he ran over someone with a truck."

Maggie took his hand in hers and squeezed. "Did they die?"

Hick let his head sink into the pillow and stared up at the ceiling. "Yeah."

She let go of his hand and draped her arm across his chest, pulling him to her. "Tell me."

He stroked her arm and took in a deep breath. "Brewster

says this boy, Thaddeus, stole the truck from a farmer he works for and then ran down a hobo."

"And the priest doesn't think he did it?"

"Honestly, Mag, the whole damned thing stinks to high heaven. The kid is shorter than Henry and it's a huge pick-up. The boy doesn't even know how to drive."

She propped herself up on an elbow and looked down at him, a wisp of hair falling across her face. "Hickory, what are you saying?"

"I'm saying I think it's obvious this kid couldn't have done it. I'm saying I don't think Brewster really thinks the kid is guilty. I think he's using him as a scapegoat."

"Oh my God," she whispered. "Why?"

"Because Thad's easy pickin's, that's why. He's colored and his family's uneducated. They got no money, and he's got no way to defend himself. He'll get a court-appointed attorney who will take the path of least resistance because a colored boy ain't worth much effort. Brewster's trying to convince the family that Thad should plead guilty. He'll go to juvenile and be out at eighteen. And whoever really did this will get off scot free." He realized his voice had risen and his entire body was tense, angry. He forced himself to relax and looked up at Maggie's face. There was pain in her eyes, pain she all too often pretended wasn't there. "You need to get some sleep," he ran a finger along the side of her face, pushing a tendril behind her ear.

"So you went to see Brewster?" she persisted.

"I made a call to the Sheriff's office to check on the boy. Brewster wasn't there, but I talked with his deputy. Thad is fine, but scared. After that I took a quick look at the truck. There was blood spattered on the grill, dented bumper and hood, busted headlight. Went to the place it happened. Whatever the hobo had with him is gone. I guess Brewster impounded all his belongings. That doesn't really matter because I have no reason to doubt that a man was run down by this particular truck right where they say it happened. It's not the place or cause of death I question. It's the driver."

"And you're sure the boy couldn't have done it?"

"There's skid marks in the gravel for a couple of hundred feet. And the truck was found in the ditch."

"And?"

"I went to see Doc, and he says the driver would have some sort of injury from the impact, that he would have been afraid and frightened and not thinking straight." Hick shook his head. "And yet somehow Thad was in bed, sound asleep the next morning, without a scratch, and went on to school without a worry in the world. It doesn't add up."

"So what can you do?"

"I don't know. I'll talk to Adam in the morning, but I don't know how much help he'll be. I'm sure he won't want me to get involved. He didn't want me to go visit the priest in the first place."

"Well, you won't be making any friends and that's a fact. Brewster's dangerous, and it could cost you your job."

"I know," Hick agreed. He turned to her, acknowledging what it might cost her as well. "What would you have me do?"

"Do you really need to ask?"

4
Saturday, July 17, 1954

"What can you do?" These were the first words to cross Hick's mind as soon as his eyes opened the next morning. Both Doc and Maggie had asked the question and he had tossed and turned most of the night trying to answer it. Now, the sun was up and Maggie's side of the bed was empty. The smell of percolating coffee wafted through the doorway, and yet the same questions that troubled him the night before were still spinning through his mind.

What could he do? What was Brewster's angle? An unidentified victim insured Brewster was not being pushed for a quick resolution by any family members, so why the rush? And why Thaddeus Burton? Father Grant had said he was never in trouble and excelled in school and even the deputy in Broken Creek knew the family and liked the boy. The eyes of Thaddeus Burton, filled with a curious mixture of desperation and resignation loomed before him.

Recalling his first run-in with Sheriff Earl Brewster did nothing to encourage Hick. Though years had passed, it still stung like it happened yesterday—Brewster's delighted picking-apart of the rookie sheriff's case. Everyone knew that Mule and Hoyt Smith were guilty as sin, but Brewster went out of his way to see they were not charged. They were kin and with Brewster blood came before justice. Hick understood Brewster had a complete disregard for truth—this was not news. But why the rush to jail anyone? Why was he in such a hurry to grab the first person he could find, someone not even physically capable of committing the crime in question?

As he pondered these thoughts, the door flew open and Jake's feet pounded across the bedroom floor while Maggie's voice was heard calling, "Jacob Prescott Blackburn, you stay out of there!"

The little boy paid no heed as he climbed onto the bed and peered into his father's face. "Daddy's awake?"

Hick pulled him close in a bear hug. "Yes, Jake. Daddy's awake."

Maggie came to the door. "Sorry, Hickory."

"It's time I got up." Hick picked the boy off and set him in the middle of the bed. He threw back the covers. "What time did they wake you?"

Maggie wiped her hands on a dishcloth. "Not long ago."

First thing in the morning and Maggie looked like she'd already put in a long day. "Is Mourning coming home today?" Hick asked.

Maggie nodded. "She'll probably go back and forth between here and Eben's for another few weeks." Mourning's brothers, Eben and Jed, had gone to fight the war in Korea.

Eben Delaney had returned, married, and recently welcomed his first child. Jed Delaney returned in a box and was buried in the National Cemetery in St. Louis. Mourning had gone to Eben's house two weeks earlier to help with the baby.

Hick stretched and walked to the kitchen. He poured a cup of coffee and glanced out the window. The sun was bright, glinting off the tin roof of the empty chicken coop. A red wasp, its thin legs dangling, buzzed at the top of the window, trying to escape. It appeared to be the start of one of those days where the heat stuck to you like a wet blanket, wrapping you up until your energy drained out. His mind wandered as he sipped his coffee and stared out across the yard. How was Thaddeus doing after another night in jail? Would his family agree to a guilty plea? How had Brewster taken the news that Hick Blackburn had stopped by the Broken Creek station. Brewster did not tolerate doubt or questioning and Hick's experience in dealing with the older man told him it wouldn't be long before a confrontation. So be it. He sighed, put the coffee cup into the sink, and went to dress for work.

The new uniform was a size larger than last year's. Age and marriage were filling out his slender frame, but he still looked young for the job. With his youthful face and slight build, men like Brewster seemed to think they could intimidate him by throwing their weight around. After the war, Hick found there wasn't much that could intimidate him, yet he knew his appearance did little to discourage people from trying.

He put his hat on and walked back into the kitchen. "I'm going on to work. You need anything?"

She spooned another helping of oatmeal into the boy's bowls and shook her head. "No, we're fine." She put the pot back on the stove and turned to him. "I hate you tanglin' with Brewster. Just be careful. I'm worried."

He crossed the room and wrapped an arm around her waist. "Don't be. Everything will be alright." He kissed the tousled heads of his sons and walked onto the porch, lighting a cigarette as he went. Taking a long draw, he watched the smoke as it evaporated into the sunshine. The trees were still, breathless, the grass beneath them brown and brittle, the sandy earth consuming the sparse blades. Even the birds seemed to move slower than usual in the already oppressive morning heat, their beaks open, their sides heaving with rapid breaths. He hesitated. Why not go back inside and have breakfast with Maggie and the boys? Why the hurry to get to work? Because work was always waiting no matter what, he supposed. Because he needed to provide for his growing family. Because he could escape into other people's problems and forget about his own ghosts. He straightened his shoulders and headed to the car.

∾

Adam's normally cheerful face was grim as Hick entered the station. He slurped his coffee and regarded Hick. "Well?"

Hick hung his hat and shrugged. "There's something off about—"

The door to the station opened behind Hick and a nervous Royal Adkins stepped inside. Shocked to see the young man in Cherokee Crossing, Hick stared at him.

"Deputy Adkins, to what do we owe this pleasure?"

Royal removed his hat and nodded toward Adam. "Morning, Deputy. Morning, Sheriff."

Hick indicated Adam and said, "Deputy Adkins, this is Deputy Kinion."

Royal stepped forward and extended his hand to Adam. "Royal Adkins. Pleased to meet you."

"What brings you to Cherokee Crossing today?" Hick asked.

Royal looked at Adam and hesitated. Catching his glance, Hick assured him. "Adam's my brother-in-law. You can say anything in front of him. Something wrong?"

Adkins gripped the brim of his hat, turning it around and around in his hands. He turned and looked out the front window.

Hick and Adam exchanged a glance and Hick turned back to Adkins and waved toward the empty chair next to his desk. "Why don't you have a seat, and tell us what's on your mind. You didn't drive all this way for nothing."

Royal sank into the offered chair and put a stick of gum into his mouth. He looked at his feet and then back toward the front door. "Sheriff," he began finally, "I been thinking a lot on what you said yesterday. I mentioned it to Brewster and he got madder'an a wet hen. He told me to put all your foolishness out of my mind and to concentrate on nabbing mail box bashers and outhouse tippers and leave the lawin' to him." He looked up and added, "I ain't bright and I own it, but there's something ain't right about this case and it's got me riled. I don't cotton being involved in wrongdoing."

Adam leaned forward. "What do you mean something's not right?"

Royal looked toward Adam and a momentary glint of suspicion flickered in his eyes. Then, he licked his lips and started in again. "It's just this ... I got to thinking about what the sheriff here was saying. About how hard it'd be for Thad to learn to drive that truck in one night. So I went out and climbed in it. I reckoned it'd be tough but pretty much figured Brewster had it right, until ..." Adkins stopped talking and cracked his knuckles.

"Until what?" Hick prompted.

"It's like this, Sheriff," Royal said, shifting forward in the chair. "There was a jar of hooch in that truck, rolled right up under the seat. It was corn liquor, and I know where it come from. Willie Taylor's been making moonshine in Broken Creek as long as I can remember and I know he's got a particular jar he uses no one else in town has."

"Could the boy have been drinking" Adam asked.

"No, sir. Miss Burton's young'uns toe the line."

"Well, what about the farmer, Sutton?" Hick asked, sitting on the edge of his desk.

"Grover Sutton is Pentecost and a deacon," Royal answered with a firm shake of his head. "He wouldn't touch the stuff."

Hick and Adam's eyes met. "Did you tell the sheriff?" Adam asked.

Royal nodded. "He told me to forget it. Said I never seen that jar and just to forget all about it." Royal looked at Hick. "How am I supposed to do that? I sit in that jail with Thad all day long. Brewster says Thad's fine and not to worry about him, but I heard him crying last night when he thought I was asleep. He ain't fine at all. He's scared. I've known him since he was a little boy. His mama done up our clothes for years and he'd run the basket of 'em to us when she was done. He would never take anything extra when we offered and his mama taught him right from wrong. The Burtons is good people. I reckon I can believe Thad might have borrowed a truck to go for a ride and got too scared to tell us he ran over that hobo. He's just a kid and sometimes kids do dumb things. But there ain't no way he'd drink hooch." He shook his head. "I hate to think poorly of Uncle Earl."

"Uncle?" Hick asked.

Royal shrugged. "Hell, Earl Brewster's related to most everybody in town."

Adam caught Hick's eye and shook his head. Things did not bode well for Thaddeus Burton.

Royal looked at Hick. "I pondered it and pondered it, but I just don't know what to do." He turned his hat in his hand again.

"What do you want to do?" Hick asked.

Royal sat thinking a moment. "I reckon I want to do right."

5

Saturday, July 17, 1954

Hick met Royal Adkins outside of Broken Creek later that evening and followed the deputy to a deserted dirt road. He pulled his car onto the grass and shut off the engine. Dusk crept through the dense trees and cast long shadows in front of him. Glancing in the rearview mirror, he saw nothing behind him but a long, brown line of road unbroken by any structure or sign of civilization. Peering into the woods, it was impossible to make out anything through the gloom. Lightning bugs rose from the ground, luminous and spectral. They were the only signs of life in the shrub.

He watched Deputy Adkins get out of the car in front of him. Nothing in the young man's demeanor gave him cause for alarm and, yet, to join him voluntarily, at such a secluded spot could be dangerous. Sheriff Earl Brewster's reputation for ruthlessness did nothing to calm his apprehension.

"This the place?" Hick asked, climbing from his car.

"Yeah. I usually find 'em down here in the bottomlands."

The two men stepped into the tree line. The sand was soft

and slick beneath Hick's shoes, and stagnant, musty smells wafted up from puddles of black, sandy water. Because of the season's unusual dryness, underbrush and saplings grew thick in places where the river sometimes ran. They stepped over fallen trees, gravel bars, and debris in the sunken wetlands and made their way through a muddy trickle that stubbornly stayed wet even in the drought.

Darkness fell as Hick picked his way around logs and branches. Stumbling, he looked down and realized, in that brief moment, he had lost sight of Deputy Adkins. He stopped and scanned the darkness and was surprised to hear the sound of a pistol being cocked very near his ear.

"Well, well, what we got here?" a voice behind him said.

Hick's heart jumped, and his breath caught in his throat. In the light of the waning moon he could make out two shadows. Raising his hands he began, "My name is Sheriff Hick Blackburn and I'm from—"

Royal Adkins interrupted him. "Now Dewey, why you treating my friend like that?"

"You know this fella, Adkins?"

"Yep. He's just who he said he is, and I asked him to come out here with me. Now put that thing down afore you hurt somebody."

The man called Dewey stepped out of the shadows and put away his gun. He was thin and dark and had a face that had seen a lot of hard years and harder work. He looked Hick up and down and smiled, showing spaces where teeth used to be. "Sorry 'bout the gun. We thought you might be a revenuer."

"Where's Willie's still?" Royal asked. "We need to talk to him."

"He's down closer to the river now," another voice said, and in the darkness Hick saw a younger man with light hair and eyes that gleamed against his dark skin. "Getting so water ain't easy to come by."

"I reckon that's right, Dink" Royal agreed.

"What you wanting with Willie anyways?" asked Dewey. "It's worrisome you coming out here tonight and with a sheriff. We ain't had no trouble with the law in years and we'd better not be starting."

"Just a couple of questions," Royal said. "Ya'll ain't in no bind. We're just trying to find something out about another matter entire."

Dewey and Dink exchanged glances and then Dewey shrugged. "Well, come on. Willie ain't feudin' with you."

As Hick and Royal trailed behind the men, Hick asked, "Your moonshiners always this hospitable to the law?"

"Willie and Sheriff Brewster ain't the best of friends, but I get along with 'em just fine. I don't see no point bothering 'em. They don't mean no harm. They just sell moonshine at the juke joint and use it for they own selves."

Dewey turned around and smiled. "We like to keep it on hand for malaria and the croup."

Hick nodded, smacking a mosquito whining near his ear, and followed deeper into the woods.

The familiar night sounds began to swell. The whistling sounds of peepers and the chirping of crickets joined the high-pitched buzzing of toads and the occasional trumpet of a bullfrog. From the tree tops came the mournful cry of a screech owl.

After what Hick judged to be a little more than a mile , he began to smell the acrid scent of burning wood and the tang of fermentation.

"We're getting close," Royal told him. "The air has a wang to it."

They climbed a small rise and off in the distance, beside a stagnant piece of swamp water that reflected the light of the moon, Hick saw a brightly burning fire and the shadow of a man throwing wood upon it.

Dewey cupped his hand around his mouth and sang out with the rhythmic cry of a barred owl. The shadow stopped feeding the fire abruptly and stood up. He answered back and Dewey said, "Come on. He's expecting us."

Hick followed Dewey and Dink as they led the way down onto the sandy bar where the copper still and a huge pile of firewood were partially concealed by boxes and boxes of Atlas jars. It was clear the operation was bigger than Royal let on, but Hick was not concerned with moonshiners.

Willie Taylor offered a toothless smile and a large, calloused hand. "Howdy Royal," he said shaking the young man's hand. "What brings you out to this neck of the woods?"

Then he turned to Hick. Willie had only one eye and a long shaggy beard. He was smiling, but Hick sensed that beneath his friendly exterior there was a certain brutality that would not hesitate to emerge in the face of danger.

"This here's my good friend, Sheriff Hick Blackburn," Royal said by way of introduction.

Willie squinted his eye and looked into Hick's face. Hick could smell alcohol and tobacco on his breath.

"Sheriff?" he repeated. "Where from?"

"I'm from Cherokee Crossing," Hick answered.

"Cherokee? You're a long way from home, boy." Hick nodded in answer and Willie went on. "What you doing out here?"

"He's here 'cause I ast him for help," Royal said.

Willie's eye turned from Hick back to Royal. "Help with what?"

"We was wondering if you'd let us know who you been selling to lately," Royal answered.

Willie began to laugh. The laugh grew and turned into a coughing fit that ended with Willie spitting out a wad of something Hick was glad he couldn't see. "Hell Royal, if I told you that I'd be outta business in a day."

"We don't need names," Hick said quickly.

Willie turned again to him, that fierceness Hick sensed flickered a little in his eye. "Talk fast, boy. I don't know what ya'll are about but I'm beginning to mistrust it."

"What kinds of people do you sell to mainly?" Hick wondered.

"Kinds?"

"Do you sell to business folks? Locals? Church-going men?"

Willie laughed again. "I sell to thirsty folks. Mainly men, though there are some women looking for a drink now and again. Lots of poor folks who can't afford store-bought."

"You sell to colored folks?" Hick asked.

Willie frowned and squinted his eye. "Don't do business with darkies," he said in a voice of contempt. "What's this all about anyway?"

"Just trying to figure out how an empty Atlas jar smelling like moonshine ended up in Grover Sutton's truck the night that vagrant was run down," Royal explained.

"I thought they got the boy what done it."

"Just wanting to make sure," Royal said.

Willie squinted at Royal. "Brewster know you're asking questions?"

Royal swallowed hard and blinked. "No, Willie. To be truthful, he ain't got no knowledge of it."

Willie slapped Royal on the back and howled with laughter. "I like it! I hate that son of a bitch and I wish the devil'd take his soul." He tossed another log into the flame and then coughed and wiped his mouth with his sleeve. "Brewster locked up my boy and I won't see him for three more years. Three years," he repeated in a cold voice. "I don't mind iffen my kin git put away for what they done. But Brewster knowed Hap was innocent and he knowed who done it." He took a tin of snuff from his pocket and put a pinch in his nose. Eyeing Royal, he added, "They was kin of your'n if I recollect."

"I don't know nothing about it, Willie," Royal said, with a hint of protest. "But you know Uncle Earl … he don't sit still when family's involved."

Willie's face grew red with rage and he growled, "Well, what about my family? He ever think of me and mine?"

"I'm sorry, Willie," Royal said. "I ain't saying it's right. In fact, I know it ain't right. But what can I do?"

Willie shook his head and looked Royal up and down. "That bastard's gonna get what's coming to him someday and I reckon you're as much a man as anybody to do it. You'll figure it out." He threw more wood on the fire and said, "Iffen you're wondering if that boy you got there in jail bought 'shine from me, I tell you he didn't."

"What about Grover Sutton?" Hick asked.

"The deacon? Hell no."

"You the only one around using the Atlas jars?" Royal asked.

Willie's fierceness returned. "Them's my mark. Nobody else darst to use 'em 'cause they know them's my mark. Ain't none of my people take a jar to somebody else neither 'cause once they had my 'shine they don't want nobody else's. Iffen they was an Atlas in that truck then it was my hooch, plain and simple."

"You sell much this week?" Hick asked.

Willie puffed up. "I sold dozens of jars this week. We's in the sweet spot of our run and all the county knows it."

Hick and Royal exchanged glances. It was clear they would not be able to figure out who bought the moonshine from Willie Taylor.

A large pop followed by cascading logs distracted Willie from the two lawmen. He went to the fire and quickly kicked the wood back into place and built the fire back to his liking. Turning again to Hick and Royal he said, "Iffen you ain't got no more questions, I got work here."

Royal held out his hand. "Thanks for talking to us, Willie. Be careful out here and steer clear of the revenuers."

Willie laughed. "Ain't worried. My boys there know how to deal with revenuers. You may stumble over the resting place of one or two on your way out."

In spite of his laughter and friendliness, Hick did not doubt Willie's word. He was sure Dewey and Dink had used that pistol before.

The four men turned back toward the marshy woods. The full moon was waning, but there was plenty of light to see now that it was above the treetops.

"Ya'll think you can find yer way out?" Dewey asked.

"I reckon so." Royal shook the man's hand. "Thanks for taking us, Dewey. Dink." The two men melted into the darkness as Hick and Royal made their way back through the fallen timber and thick underbrush.

Hick was grateful to see the car still parked beside the dense woods. Brushing burrs from his pant cuffs, he lit a cigarette and surveyed the lonely place.

"Sorry we didn't find nothing out," Royal said as he scraped the mud from his shoe across the gravel.

Hick fanned a mosquito away. "We may not know who bought it, but we definitely know who didn't. It's a start." He paused. "What was Willie talking about back there? He said his son didn't do something."

"It was back when I was a boy," Royal said.

"What happened?"

"Somebody broke into the general store and robbed it. They hit ol' man Johnson over the head with a bottle. He ain't been the same ever since." Royal leaned back against his car and stared up at the starry sky. "They arrested Hap

Taylor and sent him to the prison farm. I reckon it's been nigh on ten years he's been there."

"And Willie thinks he's innocent?"

"To be truthful, most folks think he's innocent."

Hick stepped in front of the deputy and looked him in the eye. "Who did it?"

Royal shrugged. "Honest to God, I don't know. There was talk it was one of my cousins, but nobody ever proved nothing."

"This seems to be a goddamned habit with ya'll over here in Broken Creek," Hick said. "Locking up the easiest pickin's you can find without any regard for truth."

"I don't like it neither. I'm hoping to take over after Uncle Earl retires."

Hick's heart pounded, and he took a long drag to calm himself. "How many other men been put away for crimes they didn't commit?" Royal looked down at his shoes and said nothing. Hick snorted in disgust. "It's time to put a stop to this."

"Tell me what to do," Royal said. "I can't stop it on my own. I only been deputy for a few weeks."

Hick closed his eyes to think. "Did you see where that vagrant was killed? Did you go to the crime scene?"

"No. Uncle Earl don't take me places like that. He took my Uncle Don. That's his brother."

"The coroner?"

Royal nodded.

"Jesus," Hick swore under his breath. "You see the police report or any of the evidence?"

Royal shook his head.

Hick ran his hand across his chin. "Brewster at the station tonight?"

"He likes to sleep at home. I stay at the station most nights."

"Good," Hick said. "We're going back out to the crime scene, and then we're gonna take a look at that report."

6

County Road 14 was a narrow line of gravel lined by ditches and enormous cotton fields that stretched to the distant tree line, beyond which lay still more cotton fields. The exact spot where the accident occurred was still obvious as the skid marks had stripped away the dark gravel to reveal the light-colored sand beneath. And where the gravel gave way to grass and weeds on the side of the road, a dark track bore witness to where the tires had torn into the dirt as the truck struggled to a stop. Hick shone his flashlight across the accident scene and stopped at the dark stain where the vagrant had bled out his last moments.

Royal stared down at the blood-stained road, and in an awed whisper said, "I didn't realize the accident occurred here. What are we looking for?"

Hick used his flashlight beam to trace the skid marks from the road into the grass. "I don't know. Anything lying on the road, anything that seems out of the ordinary."

Royal squatted to get a closer look at the skid marks.

"Looks like the driver was headed that way," Hick pointed with the light.

"That's toward Sutton's place." Royal straightened up and stepped back into the grass as a car drove past without slowing, its driver oblivious to the men standing at the side of the road, or to the dark spot where a man had died just days earlier. "This here is close to where Pack Barnes stays," he added, shining his own flashlight into a clump of scrawny trees yards away from the road.

"Pack?"

"Pack Barnes has been in Broken Creek as long as I can remember," Royal said. "I don't recollect his real name. He's lived in his Packard for so long that that's just what folks took to calling him."

"Lead the way. Let's find out if he saw or heard anything."

Hick followed Royal as they picked through the brush and toward the stand of trees. Soon they came to a clearing where a darkened car sat by a cold, blackened fire pit. They shined their flashlights through the car windows, but the car was empty. Hick knelt by a pot of pork and beans sitting on the ground next to the fire pit. The beans were dried and crusty, but a spoon was still in the pot, as if someone had been interrupted in his dinner.

"Well, where is he?" Hick asked.

"Hell if I know. He usually don't go far."

They opened the car door and peered inside. There was an extra pair of shoes, some under clothes, checkered shirts, several pairs of socks, and some denim trousers all folded neatly on the front seat. A pillow and blanket lay across the back seat and in the back window sat a plastic comb, shaving cup, and razor.

"This car run?" Hick asked.

"Not to my knowledge. I don't think its run in years."

"It's strange," Hick said, looking around him, "it looks like Pack hasn't been here for several days but wherever he went, he didn't take his things with him." He paused. "You see him since the accident?"

Royal's eyes widened. "Now that you mention it, I ain't."

Hick shown the flashlight up toward the road. "You think the fella killed could be this Pack?"

Royal drew in a sharp breath. "I sure hope not."

"You haven't seen him, but you haven't heard he left town for any reason?"

"I ain't heard nothing about Pack leaving town and that would have been big news. He's a regular fixture in these parts."

Hick shone his light around the darkened campsite and up the ditch toward the road from where the sound of another passing car could be clearly heard. "Pack do any drinking?"

"His drinking is why he's living in a Packard."

"Seems funny him up and leaving without a word …"

Royal nodded and peered into the surrounding darkness as if Pack might turn up somewhere unexpectedly.

"How's he usually get his moonshine?" Hick asked.

"He walks," Royal answered. "There's a juke joint down the road a piece where Willie sells it. It ain't far. That's why Pack settled in this spot."

"How far is Sutton's field?"

Royal pointed. "No more than a mile that way."

"And where do they sell the hooch?" Hick asked.

"Two or three miles in this direction," Royal said, again pointing.

"The opposite way?"

Royal nodded.

Up on the road, another car sped by. "It always this busy out here?"

"It's one of our busier roads."

"And you haven't heard anything about Pack going on a trip?" Hick asked again.

Royal pushed his hat back and scratched his head. "Not a word. Don't know where he'd go anyway."

"Why would he leave in such a hurry, and without his belongings? His shaving kit's still here. His bedroll." Hick pointed at the pot of beans. "Hell, even his dinner's still here. And why so secretive?" He panned his flashlight around the campsite for any clue. He gazed up toward the now-silent road. "Would it make sense for this Pack Barnes to walk a mile out of his way to borrow a truck?"

Royal frowned. "Not to my way of thinking. He ain't never done it before so I can't think why he'd start now."

Hick's light fell on a coal oil lamp tipped over in the dust. He bent down and studied it. "That's strange."

Royal knelt beside him. "What?"

"Look at this," Hick said. "The wick's not been turned down." He sniffed the air. "I smell coal oil. The lamp wasn't extinguished. It fell over and the oil leaked out."

Royal looked at Hick. "What does that mean?"

"I'm not sure," Hick said. "But I don't think Pack Barnes left his campsite for a casual trip." He rose and glanced around him. "He took no clothes and didn't extinguish his light. It was knocked over. Was it knocked over in his rush to leave, did an animal do it, or was there a struggle?"

Hick studied the dirt, but finally shrugged. "There's no way to tell. But it all seems a little off."

"Pack ain't ever been one to do things the way other folks do them," Royal said. "Maybe he just up and walked away."

"Maybe." Hick considered. "Still, something's not right about him disappearing so soon after that man was killed. If he wasn't the victim, where is he?" He pointed the flashlight into the clump of trees and looked for footprints. After a few minutes of fruitless searching, he turned to Royal. "Ask around and see if anyone knows anything. Maybe he's sick and someone's taking care of him. Check with the doctors."

Royal nodded and they continued their search of the campsite and then returned to the road and looked around for a few more minutes. "I reckon Uncle Earl picked up just about everything that was out here," Royal finally said.

"I reckon you're right." Hick flicked off his flashlight. "Let's get to the station and take a look at the case file."

The door to the Broken Creek police station squeaked on its hinges when Royal Adkins opened it.

"Who's there?" a sleepy voice called from the back.

"It's just me, Thad," Royal answered him, flipping on his desk lamp. "Go on back to sleep."

Hick squinted through the darkness and saw Thad's shadowy figure standing uncertainly at the cell door. The boy hesitated and then returned to a small cot beneath a window.

Royal pulled open a drawer from a long row of filing cabinets and handed Hick a folder. They sat at Royal's desk and Hick opened the file. The crime scene photos were gruesome and Hick struggled briefly with nausea and dizziness. He was slowly learning to deal with emotions that rose up with unexpected force—feelings so strong and vivid that often he forgot where he was. Habitually, his trembling hand reached into his shirt pocket and grabbed a cigarette. He lit a Lucky Strike and breathed in deeply, exhaling a ragged breath that he hoped Royal didn't notice.

Hick's eyes fixated on the deep, bloody neck wound, so severe the man had been nearly decapitated, fat showing through the long gash. The victim was Caucasian and thin, but his face was so swollen and disfigured that it was hard to place his age. He turned the photo toward Royal. "Could this be Pack?"

Royal shrugged. "That could be anyone."

Unable to look at the photo any longer, Hick picked up the police report and began to read.

At 0400 hours on 14 July 1954 received phone call from Mr. Grover Sutton at my residence regarding the theft of a work truck from his cotton field. Stated keys left in vehicle. Stated on previous day, Thaddeus Burton, Negro, had expressed curiosity in regards to truck.

Located truck in ditch on County Highway 14. Several yards away lay an unidentified male victim. Judging from injuries to victim and damage sustained to truck, victim was struck by vehicle. Perpetrator subsequently fled on foot. Coroner, Mr. Donald Brewster, declared victim dead at scene. Truck impounded at station for evidence.

—Sheriff Earl Brewster

Behind the report was the Arrest Record which said only: "Subject Thaddeus Burton found at Lincoln School (colored) and brought in for safekeeping to await Judge."

"The only facts in this whole file are that Sutton's truck was stolen and that an unidentified man was killed," Hick said, his voice tight. "Everything else is nothing more than wild speculation. There is no way a jury could convict on such flimsy evidence." Hick looked at the police report again. "Do you know this Sutton well?"

"Oh, sure," Royal answered. "Everybody knows Deacon Grover."

"Any reason why he'd implicate Thad? He have something against the boy or his family?"

Royal shook his head. "It ain't like Grover to tell tales. He's as honest as a preacher. I don't reckon he'd point fingers unless he was pretty sure."

"Why would he call Brewster at home and not phone you here at the station?"

Royal blushed. "Ain't many in town that have much faith in me. I reckon he figured he might as well go straight to the sheriff."

"Sutton and Brewster friends? Is there any reason to believe that Sutton would implicate Thad at Brewster's bidding?"

Royal shook his head. "Uncle Earl and Deacon Grover don't get along. Uncle Earl calls Sutton a sanctimonious piece of horse shit."

"Well, your Uncle Earl sure has a way with words." Hick took another long drag of his cigarette and then picked through the crime scene photos again, studying them closely. "Where are the victim's belongings?"

"Back in evidence. You want to take a look?"

"Yeah. Let's see what Brewster's got."

Located at the back of the station, the belongings were in a windowless room used for both storage and evidence. Royal went to a shelf and carried a box to a small table. Removing the top, he tipped the box toward Hick to show the few items inside.

"You dust any of these for prints to try and identify the man?"

Royal shrugged. "Uncle Earl just tossed 'em back here."

Considering the fact that Brewster had already manhandled the items, Hick realized good prints would be hard to come by so he dumped the items out and sorted through them. A beat-up leather satchel contained a few items of worn clothing and an extra pair of shoes, but no wallet. He flipped open a small leather notebook hoping to find identification. There was some scribbling in black ball point ink, but nothing of interest. A photograph of a young man and woman with two small children was paper clipped to its cover. "Did Brewster see this?"

"Doubtful. He didn't seem concerned with any of it."

Hick studied the picture and recalled the crime scene photo. "The poor bastard. I can't even tell if this is the guy that got killed or not. If it is, he may have family looking for him."

A thoughtful look appeared on Royal's face. "Seems logical now that you mention it."

Hick studied the rest of the items. There a hat, crushed pocket watch, harmonica, pocketknife, a couple of handkerchiefs, a compass for drawing circles with a well-used pencil in its clamp, and a Gideon's Bible. Nothing indicated where the man may have come from or what he did for a living.

"Any of this look like it could be Pack's?"

Royal squinted. "I don't think so. Pack's clothes were still in his car and he don't know how to read or write."

"This photo anyone you know?"

Royal shook his head.

"Where's the poor guy buried?"

"Brewster had him buried in the cemetery right outside of town by the train tracks. He rushed it pretty good. Didn't even embalm him."

Hick pulled the photo from beneath the paper clip. "I'm sending this in to the state police. They can check it against missing persons reports."

The personal effects lay spread on the table, random items that meant nothing alone, but together told the story of an unfortunate soul.

"Wait ... what's this?" Hick said as he noticed something

snagged in the folds of a handkerchief. He shook the hand-kerchief and a metallic object clattered onto the table.

Royal gasped and picked it up. "I've seen this before."

Hick took the item from Royal's hand. "It's a Citation Star." He squinted "Where've you seen it?"

"I think it belonged to Pack."

Reaching back into his pocket and pulling out the photo, Hick, again, looked at the family. In the background was a sign that read Memphis, Tenn., Mid-South Fair, September 30, 1951. Hick shook his head. "It sure as hell didn't belong to this guy. It's got some age to it—the newer ones are bigger. This looks like it's from World War One and this guy's not near old enough." He turned to Royal. "And you've seen Pack Barnes with a medal like this one?"

"Pack was mighty proud of it. He kept it with him all the time."

"That means Pack was near the scene of the crime. This could have just been lying around since he lives nearby." Hick turned the medal over in his hand. "We know the picture and the belongings aren't his. It's unlikely your Pack is the victim, but he could still be the perpetrator. At the very least, there's a chance he's a witness." He looked up at Royal. "We need to find him."

They shut out the light and closed the door to the storage room and Hick returned to the crime report to look, once more, at the crime scene photos. "Poor bastard." He closed the folder and handed it to Royal. "Don't say anything to anyone about us looking in here or this picture or why you're looking for Pack Barnes. Just say you noticed his car was empty and you're worried about him. I gotta get home. Besides finding Pack, talk to Sutton and figure out why he pointed the finger at Thad."

Royal's eyes shone with excitement. "You think we can do this? You think we can find this guy?"

Hick's eyes trailed to the cell in the back of the jailhouse where Thad was sitting up, listening. "I hope so."

7
Sunday, July 18, 1954

On his way out of town, Hick drove past the Broken Creek Post Office, a tavern, two cafes, and a movie theater, all closed. He stopped at the blinking red light at the town's only four-way intersection and lit a cigarette, watching the smoke drift toward the open window before continuing on. Humidity hung heavy in the warm night air, ghost-like and vaporous, ringing the moon in a gauzy film. As he turned toward the two-lane highway, he was surprised to see a car in front of the tiny Catholic Church and a light shining from Grant's office. He had decided against checking in with the priest because it was past midnight, but seeing the light on, he drove into the parking lot.

As he pulled in, he saw that a young man wearing a letterman's jacket was leaning against the parked car. Hick climbed out, tossed his cigarette to the ground, and put it out with the toe of his boot. The teenager didn't turn toward Hick or even acknowledge his existence, but instead stared intently up at the church's door. Hick adjusted his hat and started to walk in the teen's direction when angry voices inside the church caused him to pause in his steps. The church door flew open and a man Hick didn't recognize stomped down the porch and stopped in astonishment.

"Jesus Christ!" he exclaimed. "You scared the shit out of me! Who are you?"

"He's a friend of mine," Father Grant said quietly from the doorway.

The man turned and looked at the priest in surprise. "A friend?"

"Sheriff Hick Blackburn, this is Ike Davis, President of the School Board."

"Sheriff?" the man repeated in surprise. "Sheriff of what?"

"Cherokee Crossing," Hick replied, holding out his hand.

The man shook the hand extended and explained, "Sorry if I was a little rude. Didn't expect to find anyone out here in the middle of the night."

"Understandable," Hick answered.

The man hesitated a moment, looking Hick over and then said, "I best get my boy home. We need to be up early for church and the missus will be worried about us. You know how mothers are." He gave Hick a weak smile and turned back to Father Grant. "I'll think on what you said, but I reckon I know best." He paused with his hand on the door and closed his eyes. "I'm sorry." With that, he and his son got into the car and they drove off into the misty night.

Father Grant watched them leave and then said, "Won't you come in, Sheriff? I didn't expect you."

The sanctuary was dark except for a flickering candle that hung from the ceiling. Esther Burton's typewriter was covered with black vinyl and her chair was pushed under the desk. The light pouring from the office of Father Grant was the only sign of life in the stillness.

Hick followed Grant into his office. There was a still-smoking cigarette in an ashtray and the side chair was pushed away from the desk. It seemed Ike Davis had left in a hurry.

"What was that all about?" Hick asked.

Grant looked tired. There were bags under his eyes and his shoulders drooped. He sank into the chair at his desk and shrugged. "Same old story."

"There's lots of old stories." Hick moved the chair back to Grant's desk and took a seat.

"True enough," Grant said. "Seems this one doesn't have a happy ending. Broken Creek's been preparing to desegregate their schools next year. We simply can't afford to maintain two separate systems. Fayetteville and Charleston are doing it. Ike has been working on the plan for months. I thought he'd ironed out the details. The students were to be told this term so they'd be prepared for it. He had supportive teachers lined up and the PTA had been notified. Now, it seems, it won't happen … not anytime soon anyway." He shook his head. "Every time we come close to taking a step forward something happens. People are afraid of change, and it's a damned shame."

"Why the change of heart?"

Grant gazed past Hick and then shrugged. "I can't say.

Ike had instigated the whole thing. He was the one who convinced the school board to implement a plan. Said it was 'morally right' and he aimed to do it. I can't explain it."

"You know, there's never been a single colored family ever lived in Cherokee Crossing. I never even met a black man until I went into the army. The colored soldiers couldn't eat at our mess, or sleep in our tents. They were just 'attached' to our unit because the army was segregated." Hick frowned and looked into the priest's face. "But they fought and bled and died just as easy as any white man."

Father Grant ran his hand across his beard. "Broken Creek, Arkansas has always been a friendly town. White folks and black folks work together in the fields, they shop together, the kids all play together. It was just logical to mix the schools. As far as I could see most people thought it was a good idea. I hadn't heard of any real opposition."

"I wonder what happened?"

Grant answered with a look of bewilderment. "Ike came over here tonight unannounced and informed me he was publicly withdrawing his support for the plan at some rally planned for Wednesday night. It doesn't make sense. We've spent hours working on this, but I guess someone confronted him, and he got cold feet. I simply don't understand. It'll happen sooner or later. It has to." He rubbed his eyes. "Ike wants me to inform my Parish tomorrow that, in spite of what the Supreme Court says, Broken Creek will not be desegregating any time soon. He's talked to all the colored pastors tonight because he thinks delivering the news from the pulpit will make it easier for folks to swallow."

"And will it?"

"The little colored children in Broken Creek attend school in a one-room building four miles outside of town. There's no indoor plumbing, sunshine streams through cracks in the walls and ceiling, it leaks like a sieve when it rains, and it's infested with rats, fleas, and cockroaches. The older kids leave home at six in the morning to travel fourteen miles to go to another county. Nothing I, or anyone else, can say will make this news any easier to take." He frowned and set both hands on his desk as if to declare the topic closed. "Well, you didn't come here to listen to my troubles. What's on your mind?"

"I wanted to let you know you were right. Right about the boy, right about Brewster. Something stinks to high heaven about the case against Thad Burton."

"I see." Father Grant leaned back in his chair and looked at the ceiling as if he could find answers waiting for him there. "So what's to be done?"

Hick shook his head. "I don't know. I do know that whoever was driving that truck had been drinking moonshine bought at a particular still. I know the man who runs the still doesn't sell to colored folks. And I know that Thad Burton is not guilty."

"Well that eliminates one person in a town of twelve hundred," Grant said with a tired sigh. "What good is that?"

"Not much, but it's a start. There's a lot of investigating to be done."

Grant leaned forward. "The Judge returns from his fishing trip on Wednesday. Esther told me Thad plans to confess as soon as he sees the judge. Brewster's convinced the family it will be the best thing. No trial, the boy goes to the juvenile farm for six years and then he's home."

"Is there any way to convince Thad to plead not guilty or at least to stall for a couple of days?"

"Thad's daddy is convinced a plea is the only way to save his son. Brewster told Enos the courts would look at Thad as an adult if it goes to trial."

"An adult? That's ridiculous. He's just a kid."

"You ever hear of George Stinney?" Grant asked.

Hick thought for a moment, then shook his head. "Don't think so. Why?"

"He was just fourteen when the state of South Carolina executed him. The jury spent all of ten minutes before they threw away that colored boy's life. You may not have heard of him, but I guarantee you Thad's daddy has."

"You're saying Brewster intimidated the family into a guilty plea?"

"Yes. I am absolutely saying that."

"You think it'd help if I spoke with Thad's father?"

Father Grant regarded Hick. "I don't want you to take this the wrong way but, no, it won't help."

"I'd like to try."

Grant shrugged. "Enos works at the Pig Shack, a barbecue joint on the south side of town. It's a popular spot for Sunday lunch, and he'll be there in a few hours to get the fires going to roast the pigs. You can wait here. Get some shut-eye in the meantime."

"He won't be in church later?" Hick asked.

"No," Grant said with a short laugh. "Enos isn't a church-going man."

∾

As Hick approached, he saw Enos Burton hoist half a hog off his broad shoulder and slap it down onto the grill. He picked up a rake and bent to smooth the glowing embers into an even pile. Without turning or stopping his work, Enos growled, "What you want?"

"I want to talk to you about your son."

The raking stopped as Enos straightened his six-foot five frame and turned to face Hick. His skin shined with sweat and his face was set in a tight scowl. "What about?"

"I want you to tell him to plead not guilty."

Enos squinted and took a step forward. "What business is it of yours?"

Hick held out his hand. "My name's Hick Blackburn. I'm the sheriff of Cherokee Crossing."

Enos glanced at the outstretched hand but didn't take it. "What you doing in Broken Creek?"

"Father Grant called me."

Enos rolled his eyes and set the rake aside. He poured a pile of salt on his hands and began to rub it into the hog's skin. The two men were silent until Enos slapped the hog on the rump and closed the lid of the smoker with a hard thunk. He wiped his hands on a stained apron and turned to Hick. "Tell that priest I know he mean well, but he don't know what it's like for colored folks."

"I think he does."

Enos snorted a bitter laugh. "You white folks are something else. You like to pretend you know what's best for us, that you got our interests at heart. But at the end of the day you get to go home and be safe and white. We don't get to leave. We always black."

"I'm not gonna deny that what you say is true," Hick said, "but, can you at least stall for a couple of days? Tell Thad to not say anything? Buy me some time?"

"Buy you time for what?"

"I know Thad didn't run over that man. I know Brewster, and I know he set your son up. Give me a few days, and I'll try and figure this thing out."

"Why?"

"I have my reasons."

Enos stepped forward. "This is my boy. I want to hear those reasons."

"I got history with Brewster," Hick said. "Let's just say, I owe him one."

"You want me to risk my boy's life so you can get back at Brewster?"

"He won't be risking his life."

"Brewster say he will."

"You trust Brewster?"

Enos looked Hick up and down. "I don't trust you none neither."

"Fair enough," Hick said. "I can't think of a reason why you should."

Enos picked up a poker, stepped to a second smoker, and

and stirred the embers of another fire. After a moment, he turned and pointed the poker at Hick. "You just like that priest. He tell Esther the same thing. I told that girl not to take up with that religion. Why she gotta leave her mama's church, I'll never know. And now that white man telling her Thad gonna be okay. But that ain't the way it work, not for us. I can't get him no lawyer. The lawyer they'll send ain't gonna do nothing for him. Don't you understand? Iffen he don't confess and it goes to court, he ain't got a chance. Let me do what I think best for my boy. He's a good son, he helps his mama … he wants to be a preacher. If we do what ol' Brewster tell us, in six years he'll be home again. If we don't, we gonna lose him forever."

"So you'll tell him to plead guilty."

"Yes, sir. My mind's made up"

"Then I don't have much time," Hick said with a sigh.

He turned to go, but Enos called after him. "Tell me the truth. Why you messin' with this? Why can't you just leave it alone?"

Hick turned and held Enos's gaze. "Your son's innocent. He's just a boy. It ain't right."

Enos said nothing more, so Hick turned and walked back to his car for the long drive home.

8

Sunday, July 18, 1954

"Headed to the diner for coffee," Adam said as Hick stepped from the car in front of the station. "Let's talk there."

"Sounds perfect." Hick suppressed a yawn and stretched his back. "I haven't slept all night."

The bell no longer clanged when the diner's door opened and it wasn't the busy place it used to be, but Bud still brewed the best coffee in the county and business always picked up on Sundays after church.

The two men took a booth toward the back of the restaurant and waited for Jenny Williams, the new waitress, to set two cups of coffee on the table. Adam blew on his and then took a long drink. He set the cup on the saucer, and waited as Hick poured cream into his cup and took his time stirring it.

"Well, let's have it," Adam said, finally.

Hick sat the spoon down and rubbed his temples. As tired as he was, he thought Adam looked worse. Lines rimmed

Adam's red eyes, and Hick realized the night shift was taking a greater toll on his brother-in-law than it used to. "Well," he said. "Royal was right. It's pretty clear Brewster set the kid up."

"What about the moonshine?"

Hick's thumb absentmindedly caught a drop of coffee on the side of the cup. "All I can tell you about the moonshine is that the kid didn't buy it."

"How do you know?"

"I talked to the moonshiner and he—"

"You what?"

"He's not in our county so it's not like I could arrest him. Anyway, I talked to him to find out if he sells to colored folks."

"And?"

"And he's not the most pleasant man on earth. No, he didn't sell any 'shine' to that kid."

Adam leaned back in the booth and drummed his fingers against the table. "But why would Brewster frame a kid? What can he gain from it?"

"He's covering for someone. We both know he's got a long history. Maybe it's even one of his kin. Remember Mule and Hoyt and how he made sure they'd get off? There's also a missing hobo that might be the culprit. If this hobo flew the coop, it might be more work than Brewster's willing to put in." Hick shook his head. "Think about it. A poor Negro is the perfect scapegoat. Brewster is the law, so it's easy to convince the family that the kid should plead guilty. He's a minor so he won't be gone long, and since he's colored the family knows they can't assume justice. What else could it be? We know the victim's family's not pressuring him because they don't even know about the accident."

Hick reached into his pocket and handed Adam the photo found in the victim's notebook. "Brewster threw this into an evidence box without even checking the missing persons' records."

Adam took the photo, then glanced at the door, nodding his head toward it. Hick turned to see Wayne Murphy, the town's newspaperman and no friend to the sheriff's office, enter and take a seat at the counter. "I doubt the press over in Broken Creek is putting pressure on Brewster, seeing as the victim was a vagrant." Adam put the photo in his shirt pocket and sat back to make room for a plate of fried eggs and bacon.

"So, why the hurry to get Thad to—"

"We may be about to find out," Adam interrupted. "We've got company." Before Hick could even turn in the booth, Earl Brewster was beside the table.

"Gentlemen." Brewster's voice was thick with rage.

Hick looked up and motioned with his cup of coffee. "Would you like to have a seat, Sheriff?"

"No. I'll make this short and sweet, so even ya'll can understand." He bent over and placed his thick, fleshy hands on the table. Heavy jowls wobbled beneath reddened cheeks and dark narrowed eyes. "I hear you been poking around in matters that ain't your business. I suggest you keep to your own people and leave mine to me."

Adam leaned back in his seat, his demeanor relaxed and downright neighborly, but Hick knew better. "Poking around? Now why would we be doing that?"

"My deputy told me Blackburn stopped by asking a lot of questions. And, I got a witness says he's been seen with that papist again."

"A witness?" Hick repeated in surprise. "Since when it is a crime to visit someone? Father Grant is my friend, so I reckon I can visit him any time I want."

"Midnight sure is a funny time to go calling. I know exactly what you're up to. Thad Burton's sister works at that church, and I know that Catholic is trying to get folks riled up. I tell you that boy ran over that bum plain and simple, and I got all the proof I need."

"Sounds like an open and shut case, then," Hick said with a shrug.

"That's right. Thad's daddy and me had this thing buttoned up."

"Then why are you here?" Hick asked.

"I said we *had* everything buttoned up. And now you gone and found the kid a fancy lawyer." Hick was surprised and his face showed it. Brewster shook his head in disgust. "I know you talked to Enos, but hell, I didn't reckon he was stupid enough to risk getting his boy tried as an adult."

Hick set his cup down. "Brewster, I don't know what the hell you're talking about. I don't know any lawyers, and when I spoke with Enos Burton this morning, he insisted his boy was pleading guilty come Wednesday."

It was clear Brewster didn't believe him. He bent close enough that Hick could smell the tobacco and black coffee on his breath. "Listen, Blackburn, and listen close. I don't want to hear about you coming over to Broken Creek again.

I got ways of dealing with cops who don't know how the game is played, and you've been asking for a lesson for a long time. I'll be glad to show you how things are done in Broken Creek next time you come to town."

Hick held Brewster's eyes. "Sheriff, Broken Creek's not your kingdom, and I will come and go as I please. I ain't interfering in any 'investigation' you might be conducting, and I'll be damned if I let you tell me what I can and cannot do. If everything is as neat and tidy as you say it is, then go on home and stop worrying. If you got something to hide, then it's the lawyer you'd best worry about, not me."

Brewster bent over and reached toward Hick, menace written on his heavy, reddened features. Hick forced himself not to flinch, but before he realized what was happening, Adam was on his feet with a fistful of collar in his grip. He pulled Brewster toward him and growled in the man's ear. "You're gonna need a lawyer of your own if you lay a finger on Sheriff Blackburn."

Brewster pushed Adam aside, stepped back, straightened his hat, and pointed at Hick. "Consider this a professional courtesy call. Stay out of Broken Creek. I wouldn't want your health to suffer."

As Brewster stomped toward the diner door, Adam slid back into the booth and dug into his breakfast with a vengeance. Before Hick could so much as utter thank you, Wayne Murphy loomed over the table.

"Want to tell me what that was all about?"

"Just a professional disagreement," Hick said, waving the question away with his coffee cup. The last thing he or

Adam wanted was Wayne Murphy hounding them for a sensational headline.

"Disagreement?" Murphy cast a skeptical eye at Adam. "Pretty heated one, if you ask me."

"Well nobody asked you," Adam said, shoveling a fork full of eggs into his mouth.

Wayne Murphy's eyes gleamed like a kid with a secret. "Yeah, ol' Brewster's got trouble in Broken Creek, and there ain't nobody denying it."

"What do you mean?" Hick asked.

"Oh, nothing," Wayne smiled. "Nothing more than a professional disagreement, I figure."

Hick glanced at Adam across the table. Adam rolled his eyes and turned back to Wayne. "Out with it, Murphy."

Unable to contain himself, Murphy sat down and Hick reluctantly scooted over to make room for him. "Word is that kid Brewster locked up got a lawyer to come advise him. And not just any lawyer. One from some fancy firm in New York."

Adam put his fork down. "New York? How'd he manage that?"

"It's a mystery. Nobody knows where she came from or how she found out about the case."

"How do you know all this?" Hick asked.

Murphy puffed up. "I've got sources. Don't forget, the newspaper in Broken Creek is right across the street from the police station. Just like here."

"What else did you hear?" Adam asked.

Murphy clearly relished the idea that he had information

Hick and Adam wanted. It was also clear, he was unable to keep it to himself. "Word is a hired car pulled up in front of the station. An attractive, young woman in a suit exited the car, entered the station, and left a little later with Thad Burton in tow. Brewster was out the door minutes later and, judging by the time all this happened, apparently came straight to Cherokee Crossing to pay you a visit."

"How do you know the woman was a lawyer?" Adam asked.

"'Cause Royal Adkins told Butch Simmons, the reporter in Broken Creek, and he called me lickety split. Royal says this woman barged in the station and cowed ol' Brewster. Last thing on earth Brewster expected was a big city lawyer showing up at his door first thing Sunday morning. She told him she didn't think his probable cause for bringing in Thad was worth a hill of beans and that if he didn't release him to her she'd get a friend to go over to Randolph County and get a writ of habeas corpus. Said it was unacceptable to leave a minor behind bars because the judge was too damn lazy to shorten his vacation. Said Broken Creek was violating Thad's constitutional rights, and after an hour or so of that, Brewster was glad to turn the kid over to her. He told her to take the brat and go ... only to be sure Thad stayed with his father and it was on the lawyer to see to it he was at the courthouse first thing Wednesday morning for his hearing." Wayne made a great show of looking at his watch. "And as soon as she left, he got in his car and then he showed up here, like clockwork. I think he's made up his mind that you were the one who called her."

"Where are the lawyer and Thad Burton now?" Hick was already itching to go see what the hell was going on.

Murphy shrugged. "Don't know that. I assume she took him home to his daddy."

A phone rang in the back of the diner and Bud called out, "Sheriff, operator says you got a call."

Since the retirement of Deputy Wash Metcalfe, the operator had learned to track Hick and Adam, everywhere from the diner to the doctor's office.

"Who is it?" Hick asked.

"Somebody named Carol Quinn. Says she's a lawyer."

Adam and Hick exchanged a surprised glance and Hick rose to answer the call. "Don't forget," Murphy said as he slid to let Hick out of the booth. "I helped you with this one." Murphy grabbed Hick's arm. "You owe me."

"I'll let you know if I find anything out," Hick said and went to the back of the diner.

"Sheriff Blackburn," Hick said into the receiver.

"Sheriff? My name is Carol Quinn, and I'm an attorney advising Thaddeus Burton. I wonder if you could meet with me somewhere. I have some questions I'd like to ask you."

"Can you come here, to Cherokee Crossing?" Hick asked. "I'm not welcome in Broken Creek at the moment."

"I'll be there in an hour." The line went dead.

9

Sunday, July 18, 1954

Hick stood at the window of the station sipping his third cup of coffee and watching for the lawyer. He ran a finger over the film of dust that had settled on the venetian blind, then rubbed his fingers together and watched it float feather-like to the floor. The sound of gravel crunching drew his eyes back to the street and he watched a shiny, black Oldsmobile pull up in front of the station.

A young woman exited the vehicle, smoothed her skirt, and walked toward the door. She entered the station and marched straight toward Adam's desk. "Sheriff?"

Adam nodded in Hick's direction. "That's the sheriff."

She turned and let slip a surprised "Oh!"

Hick was used to it as most strangers to town still thought he was too young to be sheriff. He walked toward her and held out his hand. "Sheriff Hick Blackburn."

She leveled a business-like gaze at him and took his hand with a grip meant to impress. "How do you do? My name is Carol Quinn."

"A pleasure," Hick said with a nod toward the small side chair at his desk. Carol Quinn was not what he expected when Murphy had said a New York lawyer was on the case. Young, attractive, and dressed in a trim, dark gray woolen suit, she seemed to be trying very hard to be the big city lawyer small town folks would expect. She sat in the offered chair, removed her hat and gloves, and fluffed her blonde, short hair.

He took a seat behind his desk and met her gaze. "What can I do for you, Miss Quinn?"

She crossed one ankle over the other and placed her hat and handbag on the edge of his desk. "I understand you've been checking on Thaddeus Burton's case. I wondered if you could tell me what you found."

"I haven't found much," Hick said. "All I can tell you is that Thad didn't run over that man. I examined the truck and he could no more drive that thing than I could move a boulder by blowing on it."

"You have no suspects?"

"Suspects?" Hick leaned forward and crossed his hands. "Ma'am, that's not my jurisdiction. I couldn't arrest anyone, and I have no power, no right, to even question anybody."

Carol rolled her eyes. "Just as I thought. You people always cover for each other."

"You people?"

"Cops, you cops. You always look out for each other, make sure nobody gets in trouble no matter how illegally or brutally you act."

Adam slapped his hands on his desk and sat forward.

"Now see here, Miss Whoeveryouare—" Hick held up his hand to quiet Adam, but kept his eyes trained on Miss Quinn.

"Earl Brewster's a son of a bitch. I wouldn't do a damned thing to help him, so you best get that thought out of your head real quick. Brewster's the kind of man that makes this job tough for anyone who wants to do right. I've had plenty of run-ins with him, and believe me, I wouldn't cross the street to help that bastard."

Carol Quinn looked from Hick to Adam. "Pardon me if I'm a bit skeptical. I just spent more than an hour trying to make sense of why that fat bastard thinks Thad was involved with this in the first place. I couldn't get anything he said to make sense." She shook her head. "The man appears to be an unscrupulous, despicable human being, but I have no idea if you're being honest with me. It's hard to tell down here."

"And what the hell is that supposed to mean?" Hick made no effort to hide the edge in his voice.

"It means down here," she snapped. "Where Jim Crow is the law of the land and half of you can't read. It means here in the sticks where stupidity and illiteracy reign supreme."

Hick rose to his feet and looked down at her. "Regardless of your misguided opinions, I will ask you now to kindly leave. You may not understand or like us, but at least we know how to behave respectfully."

Carol put her hat on with an angry gesture. "I should have known better than to think I'd get any help here. But that priest ... he told me to come. For some reason, he seems to have a high opinion of you."

Hick thought of the fear in Thad's eyes when he peered out from his cell, and decided to try to keep his exasperation in check. "Where's Thad now?"

"He's home with his daddy, but I'm staying at a motel close by. His father is intent on a guilty plea. I tried to explain to him that Thad has a right to a trial by jury but his mind is made up. I plan to stay around until Wednesday and do my best to inform the family of their rights, but they don't seem to want to listen." She pulled on her gloves with a jerk. "The stupidity of it all baffles the mind."

"Perhaps, if you'd take the time to understand people, rather than running roughshod over them, you'd be at bit less baffled and a bit more sympathetic."

"You're very opinionated, aren't you?" she asked, with her head cocked.

"I deal with people at their worst moments day in and day out. I've seen enough hurt and pain to last a lifetime and something tells me that you, with your high northern ideals and your shiny black car, have no idea what it's like to feel true pain."

Her eyes narrowed. "You have no idea what I deal with day in and day out. How dare you preach at me, you ... you ... stupid hillbilly."

Hick kept his temper in check and his voice flat. "Good luck trying to piece this thing together on your own." He turned back to his desk and didn't look up when the station door slammed shut.

"Well, she's pleasant," Adam said.

Hick laughed. "Yeah, and Brewster deserves her. Let's go

ahead and look into things like we planned. Can't see as she'll be much help so there's no need to fill her in." He rose again and stretched. "I best be getting home. Maggie's probably wondering where I am."

"I'll call if anything happens, although it seems we've met our quota of daily excitement already."

"And then some," Hick agreed, with a wry smile.

Hick was unfazed by his meeting with the high and mighty Miss Carol Quinn of New York City. He had seen enough Carol Quinns in the army, people who thought they knew everything, people with a false sense of superiority, a perceived advantage over the ways and beliefs of the rural south. Her pert opinions and flat-out rudeness were nothing he hadn't experienced before, and he wasn't about to waste his time trying to change her mind.

As he turned in and followed the two dirt lines in the side yard that served as a driveway, he spied his sons seated on the porch. Their legs were straddled, their heads down, eating watermelon and letting the sticky, red juice drip down their hands to their wrists and then onto the ground between their feet.

At the sound of the car, their faces popped up and the watermelon was cast aside. They ran to Hick and pressed their dirty cheeks against the legs of his trousers. He rubbed the top of their heads and asked, "What did you learn in Sunday School today?"

"Jake slept," Jimmy said with a serious face. "But he's just a baby." At five, Jimmy would soon be entering school and felt the importance of paying attention in a classroom. "I learned that we should forgive a lot. It was more than seven times, but I don't remember the exact number."

Hick looked down at him with an affectionate smile. "I don't reckon the number is that important,"

The front door swung opened and Maggie came out onto the porch, still dressed in her Sunday best, one hand resting on her swollen abdomen. Her long, dark hair was pulled back because of the heat, and her eyes brightened when she saw Hick. There were times when his feelings for Maggie overwhelmed him, nearly choking him with emotion. This was one of them. He hopped onto the porch, wrapped his arms around her, and kissed the top of her head.

"Good morning," she said, playfully removing his hat and kissing him. "You get any sleep?"

"Not yet. Maybe I'll try and take a nap this afternoon before I go back to work tonight."

"Your sister, your mom, and all the boys are coming for dinner, remember. If you want a nap, you'd best get one now before the house explodes."

"I'd forgotten," Hick admitted as he held the door open for Maggie. He usually looked forward to Sunday dinners with his large, extended family, but this pregnancy was taking a toll on Maggie, and he'd tried to discourage her from hosting the regular get togethers. "It's an awful lot of work for you," he said, with a worried frown. "I'm sorry I haven't been much help."

"Don't be." Maggie hung his hat on a hook. "Just get some rest. They won't be here for a couple of hours."

"What about you?"

"I'm going to put my feet up and peel some potatoes. Mourning is on her way, and your sister volunteered to do most of the cooking."

"Are you sure there's not something I can do?"

"Yes, there is." She took him by the shoulders, turned him toward the bedroom, and gave him a gentle push. "Get some sleep."

With his bed before him, he realized how tired he was. It had been over twenty-four hours since he'd closed his eyes, and exhaustion pressed on him as he sat and removed his shoes. Even though it wasn't even noon, the heat in the room was oppressive. He stripped off his uniform and threw it toward the hamper, climbing on top of the bedspread in his t-shirt and underwear. He was so tired, sleep overcame him before he pulled the pillow under his head.

Suddenly, his eyes popped open. His heart pounded. His forehead was beaded with sweat. There it was again. A sound, not exactly like a shot, but close enough that it caused the blood to surge through his veins. The sound of laughter and muffled voices followed the noise and he woke enough to realize it was his nephews. He turned over and tried to catch his breath. Sounds and smells still had a way of grabbing hold of him, even after all these years. He'd be right back on the battlefield, and the stress and tension of the choices he'd made would wash over him. In those moments, it took all his self-control to stay calm.

He lay in bed another moment, but his legs longed to be moving, so he sat up, hands shaking, and reached for the pack of cigarettes on the dresser. But then he stopped.

Maggie didn't like him smoking in the house anymore. He stood, ran his fingers through his sweaty hair, and then pulled on a pair of trousers and a checkered shirt. Opening the bedroom door, the breeze from the windows in front of the house washed over him, cooling his damp forehead. He took a deep breath, and headed for the kitchen where he found Maggie mashing potatoes at the table, while his mother sat drinking iced tea. Mourning and Pam were busy frying chicken in a cast iron skillet.

"Hello Andrew," his mother said, her face lighting up when she saw him. Elsie Blackburn was the only person on earth who still called Hick, "Andrew." Andrew Jackson Blackburn was a family name, a remembrance of some distant relative who fought with Andrew Jackson way back in 1812. Even when he was a child, his mother was the only one who called him "Andrew." He was "Andy" at school until the class learned about Andrew Jackson, or "old Hickory." Hickory had, at last, been shortened to Hick, but his mother could never bring herself to call him that.

He crossed the room and kissed her aged cheek. It saddened him to see how small and delicate she had become. His father's death haunted her, but it was his mother who was the ghost. It was as if some artist was erasing her before his eyes. The lines of her eyes, face, and even her body becoming faint, less distinct with each passing day.

Pam looked up from the chicken she was frying. "Get a good nap?" Hick had always been close to his sister in spite of an eight-year age difference. Pam mothered him when he was little, and when he had returned home from

Europe a changed man, she worried over him. In fact, she was the reason Hick had applied to the sheriff's department in the first place. She figured that Adam, already a long-time deputy, could keep watch over her little brother and help guide him on a career that would keep his mind occupied on the here and now, instead of drifting back to the unspoken things that haunted him from the war.

"Kids outside?" he asked her.

"Yeah. Adam bought them a new BB gun. I'm afraid they're shooting up your chicken coop."

Hick shrugged. "Good thing we don't have chickens." Nodding to Mourning, he said, "Welcome home. We're glad to have you back."

She gave him a wide smile that lit up her face. "Thankie, Sheriff." To Hick, there was something otherworldly about Mourning Delaney. She was only seventeen, but seemed older, wiser, like some ethereal changeling. She had a peculiar beauty, not like a Hollywood starlet or even Miss Carol Quinn from New York City. Her beauty was primitive, wild, like the swamp where she was raised.

Maggie brought him a cup of coffee and peered into his face. "You get enough sleep?"

He couldn't remember the last time he'd got enough sleep. "I'm fine. Can I help you with anything?"

"No. Go and see the boys. They've been asking about you."

Hick pushed through the front door and squinted into the sunshine. He paused on the porch, sat the coffee cup on the railing, and pulled a cigarette from his pocket, cupping his hand over the lighter. He drew the smoke deep into his lungs and headed out to check on the boys in the side yard.

Danny, Adam and Pam's youngest boy, turned and ran toward him "Uncle Hick! We're shootin' at the coop!" It seemed the yard was filled with boys—Adam and Pam had four of their own and had adopted two more, Jack and Floyd Thompson, grandsons of Claire Thompson, a woman who had died in prison six years earlier. Hick's own sons rounded out the numbers and added to the chaos.

Benji, Adam and Pam's oldest, came over, a sheepish grin on his face. "I'm sorry, Uncle Hick." He didn't quite meet Hick's gaze. "I didn't think to ask if it was okay to nail the target to the chicken coop."

"It's okay. But next time, you need to ask folks before you start shooting things up."

Benji nodded gravely. "Yes, sir. I will." Then he looked up, eyes gleaming. "You want to see our new gun?"

There were days when Hick marveled at how much Benji Kinion resembled Adam. At only fifteen, he was tall, stocky, calm, and easy going like his father, and gave the impression of a much older boy. He was quick to own responsibility for doing wrong and took it upon himself to protect and look after the flock of boys that followed in his wake.

"Sure." Hick took the air rifle Jack Thompson handed him. It was a Defender and closely resembled the M1 Hick had used in the war. It felt funny in his hands, lighter than he thought it should. Quickly, he handed it back to Jack. "That's a fine weapon you have there."

"Most kids have real rifles." Jack's voice held a hint of

embarrassment. "But Mr. Kinion says unless we mean to hunt, there ain't no point in having a real one."

"He's right," Hick said. "You'd be shooting up street signs and getting yourself in a mess of trouble. Believe me, we deal with it every day."

"I guess." Jack frowned, evidently still not convinced.

Little Jake had wrapped himself around Hick's leg like he was trying to climb it. Hick reached down and picked him up and then took Jimmy's hand. He nodded toward the coop. "Let's see how you boys are doing."

The paper target nailed to the side of the chicken coop was riddled with holes, as was the coop's door and supporting posts.

"I'll bet you could hit a bulls-eye, Uncle Hick," Benji said.

Hick shrugged and put the struggling Jake down. "I'm not much for shooting anymore."

Jack Thompson shaded his eyes with one hand and looked up at Hick. "Why?"

Hick felt a hand cover his and looked down to see the understanding eyes of his nephew, Henry, trained on his face. Henry, only two years younger than Benji, was fair and slender with a much more boyish face. Built more like a Blackburn than a Kinion, he was the only one of the four boys that resembled Pam, and he and Hick had always been close.

Hick thought about Jack's question. It was hard to put into words the gut-wrenching certainty of knowing that some things can never be changed or made right, that some things, once done, can never be undone. That once a trigger is pulled, you can't un-pull it.

"A gun, a real gun," he finally said, "isn't a toy. It's something that has power, more power than most understand. It has the power to hypnotize a man into thinking he's invincible. It seduces you into thinking you have some sort of control over a situation." He looked at the air rifle. "You can learn to shoot just fine with an air rifle like that, but a real gun is only good for one thing—taking life. And once that life is gone, there ain't no bringing it back."

"Is that why you don't carry one?" Henry asked.

"Yes."

Benji's eyebrows drew together giving him a thoughtful look. "But our daddy carries one."

Despite the fact that Benji looked like a mature, young man, he was just a boy trying to make sense of the world around him. Hick put his hand on Benji's shoulder. "I'm not saying he's wrong, not by a long shot. I'm just saying that I'm not willing to kill anyone so there ain't no point in me carrying one."

"But, Daddy—" Benji began.

"Hickory," Maggie's voice called from the house. "Come on in. Dinner's ready."

Hick smiled at the flock of boys around him. "Who's hungry?" A unanimous shout answered the question.

Flicking the cigarette toward the empty coop, Hick followed the stampede to the house. Inside, the place was a chaotic jumble of seemingly starving boys, the four older ones maneuvering around Maggie and Pam who were trying to fill plates for the little ones. Hick relieved Maggie of Jake, who was hanging onto her skirt, and sat down at the table.

Maggie brought a plate for Jake and set it down in front of Hick. "You want me to fix you something?"

"Sit down and eat. Jake and I will share, won't we?" He gave Jake a hug and the boy looked up at him, nodded, and took a big bite off a chicken leg.

She turned and went back, filling another plate for Jimmy who sat in the front room with the other kids. The house quieted some once the feeding frenzy began, save periodic eruptions of laughter from the boys.

By the time Maggie sat down, Jake had almost finished. He was gnawing on a chicken leg and adamantly refusing the fried okra Hick's mother kept offering. Jake pursed his lips, shook his head "no!", and squirmed in Hick's lap. Hick placed him on the floor and he quickly ran into the front room with the big boys.

"You still hungry?" Maggie asked, beginning to rise.

Hick put his hand over hers. "Sit still. I'll get something when I want it. You eat."

"You sure?" Her eyes were puffy and she looked tired.

"I'm sure. You stay off your feet for a while."

He kissed her, rose from the table, and drifted into the front room. As he watched the boys, he imagined Thad Burton looking out at him from behind bars. Thad would never have the idyllic childhood these boys took for granted. Instead, he would live under the shadow of Earl Brewster and a world full of Earl Brewsters who believed he was trouble, destined for prison, simply because he was colored. He would grow up walking a thin line, and still even toeing that line and doing everything right wouldn't be enough.

Hick walked onto the front porch and picked up his coffee cup, its contents now cold. He started to take it inside when the squad car turned into the drive.

"You're just in time for dinner," he told Adam as his brother-in-law stepped out of the car.

Adam frowned. "I'd be glad to eat a bite, but I need to talk to Benji and Jack."

"What's wrong?"

"Got a complaint. Harrington says the boys shot up a bunch of bottles with that damned air rifle. They left glass all over a corner of his field, and he drove right over it. Now his tractor's got a flat."

"Of all places. Philemon Harrington's not the most easy going man in the world." Turning to the front door, Hick called, "Benji! Jack!"

"Yes, sir?" Benji said, opening the door with Jack Thompson close behind. Benji saw Adam and his eyes widened in surprise. "Hey, Daddy, I thought you were at work today." Adam looked down at the boys. "I got a question for ya'll, and I want the truth. You been shooting that air rifle down around Philemon Harrington's cotton field?"

"No, sir," Benji said.

Adam pursed his lips. "Boy, I never thought I'd see the day you'd tell me a lie."

Benji's mouth fell open. "But, Daddy, I ain't—"

"He's not lying, sir." Jack stepped forward. "He ain't been shooting the rifle." Jack's gaze dropped to his shoes. "I have."

"Why?"

"I got tired of shooting at those old paper targets and wanted—"

"You wanted something that would break? Make some noise?"

Hick could see Jack struggling not to fidget under Adam's questioning. "Yes, sir."

Adam sighed. "Well, Mr. Harrington drove right up on one of them bottles while he was mowing down the brush and sliced his front tractor tire. You know how much it costs to get a new one?"

"No, sir."

"Well, you're gonna find out." Jack looked up. "You're gonna work for Harrington after school every day until it's paid for. You'll probably still be working for him come October break."

"Yes, sir." Jack's voice was quiet, full of resignation. "I knew nobody drove their cars back in there. I didn't reckon on a tractor."

"Can I help him, sir?" Benji asked. "If there's two of us working, it won't take as long to pay Mr. Harrington."

"Sure. You both start tomorrow right after school. Now go on in and finish eating."

"Yes, sir," they said in unison and fled back inside, the screen door banging closed behind them.

Adam shook his head. "Damn, stupid kids."

"Come get some dinner." Hick held the door open. "There's plenty."

Adam, never one to turn down food, followed Hick inside.

10

Sunday, July 18, 1954

Hick's eyes fluttered open after snatching a couple more hours of sleep on the couch. Dusk had descended, throwing the room into shadow and softening the stifling heat of the day. The chirping of crickets outside was overpowered by the sound of laughter coming from the bathroom where Mourning was giving Jimmy and Jake a bath. Earlier Hick had laughed at the boys' appearance. After their Sunday of play, brown streaks and sticky watermelon juice decorated their arms and ran down their thin chests. Caked-on dirt rested in the little crevices of their necks, their fingernails were black, and their bare feet and ankles were covered in dust. Now Mourning likely had them covered in bubbles.

Maggie sat at the end of the sofa, a cross-stitch in her lap. Hick moved carefully, thinking she was asleep.

She turned and smiled at him. "You awake?"

He stretched and yawned, then sat up and rubbed his face. "Yeah, what time is it?"

"Eight o'clock. I was going to wake you at nine if you

were still asleep. I know how hard it is for you to sleep on that lousy cot at the station."

"You take a nap?"

"I tried."

He yawned and rubbed his face again, trying to clear the cobwebs from his brain.

"You want some coffee?"

"Is it made?"

"No, but it won't take a minute," she said, rising from the sofa.

"Come here," he told her, grabbing her hand and coaxing her beside him. "I can get coffee in town." He ran a finger along her jawline and kissed her. Her eyes were so puffy they worried him. "I want you to listen to me," he said. "I want you to spend more time with your feet up. Let Mourning take care of things. She wants to help, and she's able, but you're always jumping up when you should be sitting down."

"But, Hickory—"

"Don't 'But, Hickory', me." He pulled her fingertips to his lips. "You've only got a few more months. Mourning wants to help more, but you can't seem to let her."

"I just—" she began, but he cupped her face and kissed her.

"Do this for me. If something were to happen—"

"Nothing's going to happen."

"Please. For me. For the boys." He held her gaze, and finally felt her resistance dissolve. Her posture relaxed and her expression grew resigned.

"Alright. If it makes you feel better, I promise to stay off my feet more."

The light from the bathroom door suddenly sliced into the room and two squealing, pajama-clad boys padded across the floor and climbed onto the couch. They smelled of soap and Hick buried his nose into their hair.

"They's ready for bed," Mourning announced. "You want me to read 'em a story?" At seventeen, Mourning Delaney had finally learned to read and was understandably proud.

Maggie sighed softly, but she only said, "Thank you, Mourning. That would be nice."

The two little boys kissed Hick and Maggie and then followed Mourning into the bedroom. The door closed and the light shown beneath it. Listening, they heard her halting voice begin the story. "Five little puppies dug a hole under the f-f-fence…"

"Magdalene Benson Blackburn, you are a worker of wonders." Hick said. "I don't reckon anyone ever thought a Delaney would read so well."

"Mourning's a smart girl. She did all the work."

Hick ran his thumb across Maggie's cheek. "You'll stay off your feet?"

"Lord have mercy. I said I would."

He patted her shoulder, stood, and stretched out his back. "I need to get ready for the night shift." He left her on the couch and went into the bedroom to put on a clean uniform.

Maggie had moved to the porch swing by the time Hick finished dressing. He stepped outside, lit a cigarette, and leaned on the railing to watch the last light of the setting sun.

He glanced at Maggie and saw she was watching him.

"Do you remember the first time you asked me to marry you?" she asked.

"You mean the time you turned me down when I was leaving for the war?"

"No, silly. The first time. When we were eight."

He laughed and took a drag of his cigarette. "I asked you when I was eight?"

"You don't remember?"

"I don't remember asking. I reckon I just always assumed you'd marry me."

"Humph."

He tossed the cigarette into the yard and joined her on the porch swing. He draped an arm around her shoulders which she promptly reached up and pinched.

"Ow! What was that for?"

"For assuming I'd marry you. You were conceited, weren't you?"

He smiled and shrugged. "Maybe. What's your point?"

She took his hand and caressed it. "I don't want you to take this wrong, Hickory Blackburn, but you were a spoiled little boy."

"Well, I got what I wanted didn't I?"

"Yes, you did," she admitted. "And I'm glad of it." She kissed him, then pulled back and studied his face. She wore an odd, thoughtful expression.

"What is it?"

"You know I've always loved you. I loved you since as long as I can remember, and I don't reckon I could love you anymore than I always have. But that conceited kid, the one who played such good baseball in high school and walked around this town so cocky … he wouldn't have done a thing to help a little colored boy in another town."

"I—"

Maggie cut him off with a finger to his lips. "I have always loved you for who you are, but every day I realize how much I love you for who you've become. I know the war was hell on you. I'm not going to pretend it wasn't. But if you ever wonder, I think it made you a better man. I don't love you more now than I did before, because that would be impossible. But I respect you more than any person I've ever known. I just want you to know that."

He gathered her in his arms and held her close, feeling her heart beat and her breath warm against his neck and knowing how much he needed her. He wanted to say something, anything. He wanted to tell her that she was his reason for getting up in the morning, for living, that she was his everything, but words, especially those words were hard to find and harder to say. Instead, he whispered, his face buried in her hair. "You'd better get some rest. I need you to take care of yourself."

Maggie ran her hand through his hair and smiled. She understood the meaning behind the words. "I will," she whispered. "See you in the morning?"

"See you then," he promised and reluctantly left his wife to go to the station.

The hours always went by slowly on the night shift because so little happened in the small town of Cherokee Crossing. Since Deputy Metcalfe's retirement, Hick and

Adam had begun trading the night shift, and the disruption to their family lives was becoming stressful. It had been bad enough to be gone every third night, but every other night was tough and, although Adam seemed able to sleep on the small cot at the station, Hick slept in fits and starts.

The ticking clock, unnoticed during the day, was loud and irritating and there were times Hick had to stifle the urge to throw a shoe at it. Each click was a reminder that tomorrow would be another long and exhausting day. He had just lit a cigarette and re-shuffled the cards for another game of solitaire when the sound of an engine caught his attention. Parting the blinds with his fingers, he watched a car swerve and then finally stop in front of the station. He rose and looked out of the front door. Royal Adkins stepped out of the car, paused, and glanced around him. He held on to the car, stumbled a bit, and wove his way toward the station.

Hick opened the door and let Royal in. "Evening, Sheriff," Royal said with a slight slur.

"Why don't you have a seat, Deputy." Hick escorted him to a chair, afraid the young man might trip over his own feet. The smell of beer was thick on his breath.

Royal turned and looked at the chair and squinted. Trying to appear sober only emphasized his drunkenness. He held both of the chair's arms and gingerly lowered himself onto the seat, with a pleased look on his face as if it were some great accomplishment to sit down.

"It's a might late to be out visiting," Hick said sitting on the desk in front of Royal.

"I reckon it is," Royal agreed and plopped his hat on the desk.

Hick waited, hoping some information as to the point of the visit would be forthcoming, but after a few seconds, finally asked, "Is there something I can do for you?"

Royal shook his head and swayed a little forward in the chair, almost falling onto the floor.

Hick was tired. Irritably, he rubbed the bridge of his nose and then his eyes. "There something you want to talk about?"

"I want to see it," Royal slurred.

"What?"

"Them people."

Hick leaned forward. "What are you talking about?"

"No, listen. I want to take a look at 'em," Royal reached into his pocket and worked to fish out a piece of paper.

Hick closed his eyes and counted ten. "Royal, you're not making sense. What do you want?"

"That fella what got killed. That vagrant. He's got people looking for him just like you said. Here."

Royal held up a crushed piece of paper and Hick took it from his hand. It was a Keep On the Lookout Bulletin from the Carroll County Sheriff's Department. On the paper was a photograph of a man and young woman.

"Where did this come from?"

"Mail. Brewster tossed it in the trash. I told him, I said, 'Uncle Earl, that might be that fella what got run over.' But Uncle Earl just shrugged and said the asshole should've stayed offen the road."

Hick glanced at the woman beside the man in the picture. It was a photo booth shot and if it was the same couple pictured with the two kids on the picture from the evidence box, this photo would be several years old. He crossed the room to Adam's desk, opened the drawer, and pulled out the picture he'd given Adam at the diner. Setting the pictures side by side, he turned on Adam's desk lamp and studied them.

Royal continued, hardly noticing Hick had moved. "Then I said, 'Uncle Earl why you got to be so damn hard all the time. What iffen that lady's looking for her man? It ain't right that she might be home worrying and not knowing.'" Royal shook his head. "It ain't good for a woman to lose her man and never know what become of him. It ain't good at all."

Hick looked closely at the pictures. Finally, he said, "You're right, Royal. Same couple. Says her name is Janice Hayes and the man's name is Claude Hayes."

"Claude Hayes. Sounds like a nice fella."

"And Brewster didn't pay any mind to this?"

Royal closed his eyes and shook his head. "Anything like that goes straight to the trash these days. He says he got other things on his mind right now."

"What could be more important than doing his job?"

"I asked him that very question," Royal said pointing his finger and leaning forward. "He told me to shut my mouth and keep it shut or I'd be back in the fields where I belong. Said there's things at work that ain't my business and iffen he didn't need someone to sit around and answer phones

he'd have already taken my badge and gun." Royal thumped
his chest where his badge was pinned. "And another thing.
I asked him if he knew anything about Pack Barnes and he
told me Pack's gone."

"Where'd he say he went?"

"I asked him. I said I noticed his car was there but Pack
wasn't and Uncle Earl told me not to worry about Pack no
more. I said Pack might be in trouble and maybe we ought
to look for him, and Uncle Earl told me to never mention
that man's name again. He said for me to shut my trap and
let him run the town as he sees fit. Told me I ain't nothing
but a dumbass anyway and that he only hired me 'cause my
mama begged him to."

Royal rose quickly and swayed. "I ain't bright and I own
it. But I know right from wrong. I know it ain't right to let
some poor woman cry her eyes out wondering where her
man is, I know it ain't right that Pack up and disappeared,
and I know it ain't right to throw poor ol' Thad in jail." He
stepped backward and tripped, almost falling over the chair.

"Come on, Royal," Hick said, putting an arm around
him. "You need to sleep this off and I don't want Brewster to
find your car here. He can't ever find out you've been talking
to me, you hear?"

"I know it." Royal looked at Hick as if he wondered
when he'd gotten there. "He's really mad at you right now."
He stumbled forward, then caught himself. "We gonna let
that woman know about her man, ain't we?"

"Sure, Royal," Hick assured him. "We'll make sure she
finds out."

"'Cause she needs to know," Royal continued in a slurring voice as Hick half drug him out the door. "It ain't right for her to not find out."

Hick helped Royal to his car and put him in the passenger seat. He opened the driver's door and pushed the beer bottles onto the floor, where they cascaded into a heap. Royal's head lolled against the passenger window. Hick drove the car to his house and pulled it in back where it couldn't be seen from the road, realizing how tired he felt and how much he dreaded the walk back to the station in the clammy night air.

"C'mon, Royal," he said, with an edge of irritation. "Let's get."

"Where are we?"

"My house. You can sleep this off on the couch. You ain't fit to drive."

His head swayed a little and he closed his eyes. "I know it." A funny smile slid across his features followed by a knitted brow and a frown.

Hick helped him out of the car and onto the porch. Quietly, he opened the door and ushered Royal to the couch. "Lie here," he whispered, kneeling beside him. "I got to get back to the station, but I'll come by in the morning."

Hick rose and bumped into Mourning Delaney who had materialized out of nowhere. "Christ, almighty!" he said. "I almost stepped on you."

Mourning's eyes were wide and she stared at Royal. "He's a little green, ain't he?"

Hick turned and looked at Royal, who was by then sound asleep. "Yeah, Mourning. He is a little green."

II

Monday, July 19, 1954

Rays of the early morning light shone on the house as Adam and Hick pulled into the driveway. The first thing to greet Hick as he walked inside was Maggie standing beside the stove, arms crossed. The boys sat at the table wide-eyed, and Mourning stood before the bathroom door from behind which a horrible retching sound emanated.

"There's a strange man throwing up in my bathroom," Maggie said. "I hope you know something about it."

"It's that deputy from Broken Creek." Hick crossed the room and banged on the door. "Royal. You okay?"

"I reckon not," was the answer, followed by a cough.

"Open the door."

Hick heard the toilet flush and then the water of the sink. Finally, the door opened and Royal's face emerged, pale and sweaty. "You look like hell," Hick said as Royal stepped into the hall.

"I feel like hell." Looking toward Maggie in the kitchen, he added, "Pardon my language."

"Here," Maggie said, handing Royal a glass. "You're not the first cop I've had to give one of these to."

Her laughing eyes met Hick's and a blush crawled up his neck and colored his cheeks. He recalled a morning in the diner when she'd handed him a glass of tomato juice mixed with some mysterious ingredients. Her look was a pointed reminder that it hadn't been that long ago when he'd been young and stupid.

"Adam's outside. Let's step out and get some fresh air," Hick said, as he ushered Royal to the porch.

Royal sat heavily on the porch swing, took a drink, and grimaced. "What is this?"

Hick shrugged. "I have no idea.'"

Royal took another long drink and wagged his head back and forth. "Christ, I'm an idiot," he said to no one in particular. Then he looked up at Hick. "What about that picture? We're gonna let that lady know, right?"

"We think it might be best to put off sending word to Carroll County for now," Hick said.

Royal stared. "Why?"

"Because Brewster will know you contacted them," Adam said, sitting on the porch rail and looking at Royal with a mixture of sympathy and annoyance. "We haven't got the bulletin here and we can't have seen that picture, so we can't do it ourselves. You'd be done for."

"I don't care about that," Royal said.

"But we need you there. Until we get this thing with Thad figured out, we need you in that office keeping an eye on Brewster. You understand?" Adam said.

Royal thought it over and nodded. "But we will tell her what happened to her husband?"

"Yes," Hick promised.

"Speaking of Brewster, don't you need to be getting into work today?" Adam asked, sniffing the bacon-perfumed air.

Screwing up his face, Royal finished his drink and gagged. "No, sir. Sheriff Brewster asked me to take the day off. Said he had some real lawin' to do, and I'd just be in the way."

Adam and Hick exchanged glances.

"He tell you what that might be?" Hick asked.

"No, sir. He just made it clear he didn't want me around."

Hick lit a cigarette and stared down the road. "You think you might be able to go into work for some reason today?"

"What do you mean?"

"I mean just stop by. Maybe you forgot something?"

"I didn't forget nothing."

Hick heard Adam sigh, but just said, "Maybe you could pretend you forgot something. Like your watch or a pocket knife?"

A light seemed to go on in Royal's mind. "Iffen I had decided to go fishing I would need my knife and it's in my drawer."

Hick nodded. "Good, Royal. That's good. I'm just curious what kind of 'lawin' Brewster's doing that he don't want you around."

Royal rose quickly, swayed, and then sat back down, pale-faced and clearly nauseated.

"Here," Mourning said, pushing open the door to offer Royal a piece of toast.

"There enough of that to go around?" Adam asked.

"Come on in and eat, boys," Maggie called from the kitchen. "It's ready."

Hick and Adam stood. "Best you stay out here," Adam said.

Royal took a tentative bite of toast and waved them away with a groan.

∿

Hick's legs jerked and his eyes flew open. He'd fallen asleep at his desk again. He shook his head and stood up, trying to muster enough energy to make it through the long afternoon. Glancing at Adam, he saw his brother-in-law was sound asleep with his feet on his desk and his chin on his chest. The heavy July heat in the station did nothing to help the two sleep-deprived lawmen.

Closing the door behind him, Hick walked out into the sunshine. A dog lay panting on the sidewalk in the shadow of a storefront, and all was quiet. He crossed the street and opened the door to the diner. Hank Williams was singing softly on the radio and a few townsfolk were having a late lunch, but hard times in Cherokee Crossing had taken their toll on the town, and the place was less than half full. Hick sat at the counter and Jenny Williams quickly approached.

"What can I get you, Sheriff?"

"Can I get a couple of cups of coffee to go?"

"It's brewing right now," she said. "It'll be a minute."

She left to try and hurry the coffee along and Hick lit

a cigarette. He turned the flint wheel on the lighter and looked into the flame, as if in a daze, too tired to think about anything.

The door opened and Hick turned to see Wayne Murphy coming toward him.

"You got anything for me?" Wayne asked as he settled on the seat beside Hick and pulled out a handkerchief to wipe his brow.

"Not yet," Hick said. "We're working on it, and I'll keep my word to you."

"I might have something for you." Wayne motioned to Jenny for a coffee. "You ever hear of the Citizens Against Desegregation movement?"

Hick shook his head.

"I didn't think you would. It's a newly organized group of so-called concerned citizens. They say they're against the federal government infringing on states' rights. Here in Cherokee Crossing, we don't pay much attention to the troubles going on around the south 'cause, let's face it, we don't have any colored folks here."

Jenny Williams brought the two cups of coffee, and Hick handed her some change. "Go on," he said to Murphy.

"According to Butch Simmons, my reporter friend, there's a newly organized Citizens Against Desegregation group in Broken Creek, and they've bought advertising space in the paper for some big rally for Senator Richardson's gubernatorial bid."

"Richardson?" Hick repeated. "I thought he was in favor of desegregation."

"Spoken like a true innocent," Murphy said with a wave of his hand. "Richardson is first, and foremost, a politician and this is a close primary. He's a state senator with aspirations to be governor and maybe president one day. The minute he figured out he had a better chance of getting voters out to the polls by being against Brown vs. Board of Education, he changed his mind."

Hick pondered this new information. "But why would Broken Creek form an organization like that? I heard they were largely in favor of desegregating."

"They *were* in favor. There's a lot in play here and a lot of pressure being put on the townsfolk. Broken Creek is important because it's Richardson's hometown, and he needs the good citizens to rally to his cause. After all, if you're running on a segregationist platform and your very own hometown is desegregating …" Jenny Williams brought Wayne a cup of coffee and he fanned a fly from it before taking a gulp. "Besides," he continued, "they needed a place in this part of the state to hold a rally, and recent events in Broken Creek made it an interesting, if not favorable location."

Hick's heart stopped. "What are you saying?"

"I'm saying that a colored boy running over a white man could not have happened at a better time for the segregationists. There's gonna be trouble in Broken Creek, and I don't reckon their esteemed sheriff will give a tinker's damn about it."

"Son of a bitch!" Hick wondered where Royal was.

Wayne put his cup down and swiveled on the stool to

face Hick. "Listen, Blackburn, I know you don't like me none and, frankly, I'm not that crazy about you. But I think we both know what the future holds. The Supreme Court said desegregation is the law of the land, and you know how some folks are down here. Damn Eisenhower. He can't make up his mind how to enforce the law, but I guarantee if he don't do something, it ain't gonna happen peaceable. People don't like to be told what to do, and it don't take much to rile 'em up or convince them that they're the victims, that change is going to threaten their way of life. That their women are in danger. Stir up just enough self-righteous anger and normal law-abiding citizens can turn into an angry mob pretty damn fast. There's gonna be news around here, lots of news. And, for once, I'm at the right place at the right time to report it."

"Damn bad timing for my little friend in Broken Creek." Hick shook his head. "They twist what happened, get people upset, and his chances of getting a fair shake shrink by the minute."

"That's a fact," Wayne agreed. He drained his coffe in one gulp and stood. "Don't forget. You owe me."

"I won't," Hick said. Wayne turned to leave and Hick called out, "Hey, Murphy?"

The reporter turned.

"Thanks."

Wayne Murphy nodded and walked out the door as Hick grabbed the two paper cups of coffee and strode back to the station. Adam's snoring greeted him and he slammed the door.

Adam shot up. "Wha…?"

"You're going to want some coffee." Hick set a cup down on Adam's desk.

"Why?"

"We may have bit off more than we can chew."

12

Monday, July 19, 1954

The afternoon passed with no sign of Royal Adkins. Hick paced from his desk to the front window and back to his desk. "Where the hell do you think he is?"

"Let's hope he's fishing," Adam said.

Hick lit a cigarette and shook his head. "I don't like it. Not one bit."

"Hell, I never knew you to care one way or the other about anything Murphy has to say. He likes to stretch the truth, you know that."

"I know," Hick agreed. "But this time everything he says rings true."

"Why?" Adam asked. "You saw the reaction here in May when the papers came out about Brown and the Board of Education. No one cared. No one said a word. Towns in Arkansas are already desegregating and everything's fine. People are generally peaceable. You're worrying for nothing."

Hick took a drag of his cigarette and turned back to the window. "You may be right. But something doesn't feel right. I got a hunch … a feeling in my gut that this time Wayne's on to something."

"Because of Brewster?"

"He's just the kind of bastard to get folks worked up over nothing. He's unprincipled and likes a little excitement. He'd think getting the town all lathered up would be fun." Hick shook his head. "His idea of fun and mine aren't the same."

"Don't borrow trouble," Adam cautioned. He checked his watch. "It's late. Go on home, and I'll let you know if I hear from that Adkins kid. I expect he just forgot to check in."

Hick rose and grabbed his hat. "Maybe," he answered, unable to hide the troubled look in his eyes. "Call if you need me."

Adam put his feet up and settled in for a long night. "Don't worry. Either he forgot all about us or there was nothing going on with Brewster worth talking about. Get some rest. You look a little rough around the edges."

Hick laughed and stepped outside. The shops were closing up for the night. People were headed home from work. It was a relaxed feeling at the end of the day when commerce was put aside for family. He wondered how much it would take to tip the scale from peacefulness to riotousness. How delicate was the balance?

He began to walk to his car when a truck came down the street and stopped in front of the station. Philemon Harrington opened the door and yanked Benji out, Jack following behind. "Kinion in there?" Harrington demanded.

"What's going on?" Hick asked, surprised to see Benji with a bruise on one cheek and a rip in his shirt.

Adam appeared in the doorway and Hick had never seen him look larger or more terrible. "What the hell happened?" His narrowed eyes flit back and forth between Harrington and his son.

"Your boy here got in a fight. First day out in the fields! I ain't got time for this, Kinion. I got cotton that needs chopping and iffen he's just gonna start trouble, he can damn well stay home." He looked at Benji. "You come back tomorrow planning to work and stay outta trouble or don't come back at all!"

He stomped around the truck and climbed in, slamming the door. The truck sprayed gravel as he drove out of town.

Adam stared at Benji. "You want to tell me what happened?"

Benji looked down, sullen and embarrassed. Jack spoke up. "Mr. Kinion, some guys came by the fields and called you and the sheriff 'nigger lovers'. They said you was helping Thad Burton get away with murder."

Adam caught Hick's eye. "How'd they—?"

"And they was handing out these." Jack reached into his pocket and pulled out a flyer. Adam took it and his face darkened. He handed the paper to Hick. It read:

GOOD CITIZENS OF ARKANSAS!
There is only one force that can prevail in the face of governmental tyranny, and that is the power of an intelligent, responsible, free community of citizens unwilling to surrender their rights to a judiciary bent on destroying their way of life. We rely on the good sense and decency of every resident in the south,

to stand enmasse against a corrupt, godless government forcing the integration of the races. This is only the first step in destroying a way of life that we, as southerners, have cherished and held dear for decades.

Senator John Wesley Richardson, Democratic Candidate for Governor will hold a Town Hall meeting in Broken Creek, Arkansas on Wednesday, July 21, 1954 at 6:00 p.m. to listen to your concerns about this blatant overreach by the Federal Government.

"Where'd these guys come from?" Hick asked, folding the paper and putting it in his shirt pocket.

"I don't know, Uncle Hick," Benji replied. "But when they found out who me and Jack were, they started talking bad about you. Saying that you and Daddy was helping that boy get away with killing a white man."

"And then what?" Adam's voice was tight with rage.

"Then I told one of 'em he was full of shit and knocked him down," Benji replied.

"How'd the rest of the choppers react to the flyer?" Hick asked.

"I don't reckon they knew what to think," Benji said. "They just read it and stuffed it in their pockets, but ol' man Harrington came out right when I knocked the fella down. Those guys all scattered and ol' Man Harrington didn't ask no questions. Just said he don't allow no monkey business out in his fields and marched us to his truck and brought us here."

"He knew nothing about the flyer or what caused the fight?" Adam asked.

"Not that I know of, sir. And neither one of us said a word on the drive over here."

"I'll talk to him. We don't need this kind of crap coming into Cherokee Crossing. I won't stand for it, and I'll tell him he'd better keep a better eye on what's going on in his fields."

"Should we go back tomorrow after school?" Jack asked.

Adam put his hand on his adopted son's shoulder. His expression was troubled. "No. Not tomorrow. I'll talk to Harrington and square this away. Just keep out of trouble, you hear?"

Both boys nodded. "Yes, sir."

"Okay, run on home," Adam said. "Tell your mama not to worry. I got this under control."

Adam frowned and adjusted his belt. His eyes met Hick's. "You may be right about trouble coming."

"After you talk to Harrington tomorrow, check in with Matt Pringle, Lem Coleman, and some of the other farmers out on Ellen Isle and tell 'em to be on the lookout. The last thing we need here in Cherokee Crossing is outside agitators starting trouble."

Adam nodded. "Will do. Now, you get on home."

The uneasy feeling gnawing at Hick didn't give way until he saw Maggie sitting on the front porch swing.

"I see you're off your feet," he said. He sat beside her and gave the swing a nudge to get it going again.

"I'm just a little tired and have one of my headaches. Mourning's frying some pork chops."

"Sounds good. The boys behave today?"

She smiled. "Of course they behaved."

He looked into her face. "And did you behave?"

"I did just what you said. I sat around and did nothing all day long. Are you satisfied?"

"Yes." He kissed the tip of her nose and pushed a tendril of hair off her forehead. "Yes, I am."

"Supper time," Mourning called from the house.

Hick helped Maggie to her feet, opened the door for her, and started in after her, the aroma of pork chops making his stomach growl. But he turned when he noticed the squad car speeding toward the house. "What's wrong now?" he muttered. Striding down to the drive, he waited as the car came to a stop.

"It's Thad and that lawyer," Adam said through the open window. "They're gone."

"What do you mean ... gone?"

"I mean I just got a call from that preacher. Thad's sister says they just disappeared. Both of 'em."

"Dammit! You think she took him somewhere?"

"I don't know, but we've got to go. I told the operator where to find us. That preacher wants to see you. Says Thad's daddy is mad as hell."

❧

"What the hell did you do with my boy?" Enos Burton demanded in an angry, but controlled voice as soon as Hick and Adam opened the door to Our Lady of Sorrows. "I told you to leave well enough alone. Why you gotta mess things up?"

"I don't know what you're talking about," Hick said. "I haven't done anything with Thad and have no idea where he is."

"But you called that lady lawyer," Enos protested. His eyes snapped with barely controlled fury. "She's the one getting everyone riled up."

"I did not call her and have no idea who did," Hick said.

"Then how did she find out?" Father Grant asked in surprise. "I assumed she found out from you."

"No, I don't know any lawyers. Especially in New York."

"You didn't call her?" Adam asked the priest.

"I did not," Grant replied, looking at Adam with a hint of distrust.

"This is my deputy and brother-in-law, Adam Kinion," Hick said by way of introduction. "So how could she have found out? Newspaper?"

"Perhaps," Father Grant answered. "The story was in the paper, but how would the local paper get to her in New York?"

The door to the church swung open, and everyone turned to see Royal Adkins enter, a sheepish look on his face. "Didn't expect to see a crowd in here." He turned to Hick. "I saw your car out front, Sheriff. What's going on?"

"Thad's gone missing."

"He's not missing," Royal said.

Enos Burton walked over and looked down at Royal. "Where's my son?"

Royal, who seemed intimidated by Enos' size, blurted, "I got everything under control." Turning to Hick, he added, "Ya'll didn't need to make a trip out here. I was on my way back to Cherokee to see you."

"Where's Thad?" Father Grant repeated.

Royal was clearly confused by the anxiety in the church. "I don't know what everyone's so worked up about. I went to the station just like you and the deputy told me to. I went to the back door and heard some voices inside. Brewster was telling a group of men he was gonna re-arrest Thad and drive that lady lawyer out of town."

"Who was in this group?" Hick asked.

"They was all our nice, respectable folks. Some of our more prominent preachers. The banker was walking out the front door."

Adam frowned and glanced at Hick. "How was Brewster planning to get rid of the lawyer and re-arrest Thad?"

"Didn't hear any particulars. Just heard Uncle Earl say that woman lawyer been meddlin' down here long enough and it was time to send her home. Said after they got rid of her they could get Thad back where he belongs and get Mr. Enos Burton to convince his boy to confess, just like they planned. Since Thad was told he had to stay at home, that's where Uncle Earl was headed. I figured it might be for the best if he and that lawyer laid low for a while. You know, someplace Brewster and those men wouldn't think to look."

"Well, where are they?" Hick asked.

"Someplace respectable folks don't go," Royal replied.

13
Monday, July 19, 1954

The sounds of music and laughter blasted through the darkness of trees that crowded around the river. A blinking sliver of light was visible at a distance as Royal parked behind the long row of cars that lined the side of the dirt road.

Hick, Adam, and Royal stepped from the car into the dense shadows of trees and Hick spied several stacked cages. From these cages came the sounds of crowing, clucking, and the flapping of wings.

"Cock fighting?" Hick asked, brushing away a mosquito whining near his ear.

"Cock fighting, dancing, a little drinking. It's your typical juke joint."

The lawmen picked their way through the underbrush toward the noise. The air had a sour smell and waves of high-pitched whirring from cicadas and crickets rang in Hick's ears. The peep of frogs swelled and then diminished as they drew near. A stick cracked and suddenly a shadowy figure loomed before them.

"Who's there?"

"It's me, Dewey," Royal answered. "I brought some friends."

Hick heard the sound of a gun un-cock, though he had never seen the pistol. Dewey approached and squinted at the men. "I recognize you," he said to Hick, "but who's the big one?"

"This is Adam," Hick said. "He's my brother-in-law and my deputy at Cherokee Crossing."

"Hellfire, we ain't never had so many lawmen out here," Dewey said, with a scratching laugh. Turning to Royal he said, "That she-devil you brought has been nothing but trouble since you left her. Dink and Willie need me at the still but I've been stuck here keeping her quiet. You owe us."

"I was afraid she might be a little hard to handle, but she wouldn't listen to me. I tried to explain to her what I was doing, but she argued with me the whole way out here." Royal said as way of apology. "The only reason she came in the first place was I had Thad with me. I didn't know where else to take them, but I knew Uncle Earl would never come looking for those two out here."

Dewey spat tobacco juice and wiped his mouth with his sleeve. "She was bothering the customers," he said. The men made their way through a clearing filled with revelers laughing and drinking. They passed more cages with roosters awaiting their fate inside the barn and beside these cages several groups of men were drinking and smoking. A shout followed by some shoving drew their attention and two men began to circle one another with their fists clenched.

Squinting through the darkness, Hick was surprised to see that Hoyt Smith was among the spectators, making wagers on the fight. Just before they turned the corner, Hick heard the thud of a fist and a groan. He turned and saw a man fall to the ground amidst cheering and dollars changing hands.

They came to a small shed behind the barn. Opening the door, Dewey said, "We had to shut her up."

The three lawmen entered the shack and were greeted by the frightened face of Thad Burton and the angry eyes of Carol Quinn, visible over a kerchief tied tightly over her mouth. She jerked at the ropes that held her hands tied to the arms of a chair, and when she saw Hick she let loose a muffled, unintelligible barrage of anger.

Hick rushed to Carol and began untying her hands. "Did you have to tie her up?"

"She won't sit still, and she won't shut up," Dewey explained with a shrug. "If I were you I'd leave her as she is."

"Christ almighty, Dewey! You can't—" As soon as one hand was loose, a smack landed across Hick's face that caused him to see stars.

Dewey laughed. "I told you to leave her."

"You stupid idiots," Carol sputtered, struggling to untie her other hand and pulling the gag from her mouth. She rose from the seat and slammed the kerchief to the ground.

"See what I mean?" Dewey said, his hands held upward in appeal.

Carol Quinn's eyes narrowed and her lips twitched with fury. "How dare you kidnap me and imprison me in this shack?" She poked Hick in the chest as she spat the words.

"I'll have the law—" She stopped, and looked at the three lawmen in front of her.

Royal stepped forward. "Ma'am, it's like I tried to tell you, I put you here for your safety."

"For my safety?" she snapped. Her eyes met Hick's. "Am I right in guessing this was your idea?"

"Your safety isn't my concern," Hick answered. He looked down at the boy beside her. "Thad's is."

Carol's eyes flitted from Hick to Adam, to Dewey, and then back to Royal. Sighing, she said, "Would someone please tell me what this is all about."

Royal looked at Hick, pleading for help. With a shrug, Hick said, "Ma'am, something's off about this whole thing here with Thad."

Her eyes trailed around the shack and then returned to Hick's face. "What do you mean by 'off'?"

"Brewster, the sheriff of this town. I tried to tell you, he ain't exactly what you'd call … honest."

Dewey snorted.

"And I suppose you are?"

Hick removed his hat and wiped his brow with his shirt sleeve. "Ma'am, with all due respect, I don't give a damn what your opinion is of me. I didn't call you, I didn't put you here, and I don't care if Brewster locks you up and throws away the key. But Thad here, he ain't done nothing wrong. I'd like to know why Brewster is so intent on locking Thad up. Why the rush to scapegoat? Why was he in such a hurry that he grabbed a kid physically unable to do what Brewster says he did."

"Hold on," Carol said, putting her hand up. "What do you mean scapegoat? Are you saying Brewster knows Thad is innocent?"

"That's exactly what I'm saying."

"But why would—?"

"I don't know," Hick said. "But I aim to find out."

Carol's anger seemed to subside. "And how do you propose to do that?"

"With a lot of work and a little luck."

"And in the meantime?"

"In the meantime, I'm taking you and Thad back to Cherokee Crossing for a night or two. I know it violates the terms of his release, but Brewster ain't too concerned with doing things by the book so I reckon we can't be either." Hick gave Adam a questioning glance.

"We could sneak them into the back room of the jail," Adam suggested.

"Jail?" Carol's voice rose an octave. "You want me to stay in the jail?"

"Well, would you rather stay out here?"

She looked around the dark shack. "No, I would not. Can't we just go to my motel?"

Hick shook his head. "You just don't get it, do you?"

"What?"

"Earl Brewster can be dangerous to tangle with, and he's got a lot of important friends. He had a carefully laid plan to get Thad to take the blame and confess to running over that vagrant, then you appeared out of the blue and put a wrench in it."

Carol frowned. "But it's all nonsense. Why would Thad confess? There's not one shred of evidence that points to his involvement in this crime. Not one."

Hick shrugged. "That may be true, but Brewster needs that confession, and he doesn't care what he has to do to get it. I don't know why he wants Thad to take the rap, but he knows if this case goes to court, there's a chance he'll be found not guilty."

"A chance? There's no way in hell a jury would convict on the evidence Brewster showed me." Incredulity laced each of Carol's word.

"Depends on the jury," Hick said. "Folks have been known to overlook little things like the fact Thad couldn't see out of the windshield, let alone that he wouldn't have the strength or knowledge to drive a truck. When it comes to colored folks, there's no guarantee a jury will do the right thing. But I don't think Brewster is willing to gamble. If he can get rid of you, get Thad back into that jail cell, and remind Thad's daddy of the desirability of a guilty plea, all before the prosecutor and judge get back from their fishing trip, then his plan will be back in order. Tidy and neat."

Carol was visibly shaken. Hick could see her thinking. She looked up into his face, the cocky defiance shattered, and asked, in a small voice, "When you say if Brewster can 'get rid of me,' what exactly do you mean?"

"Let's get you out of here and not worry about that right now. We've already had one person disappear. We don't aim to lose anyone else."

"Already had one person disappear?"

Hick ignored Carol and turned to Thad. "I'm taking you to Cherokee Crossing with me. You're going to the jailhouse, but you're not in any trouble, you understand?"

"Yes, sir."

"We're gonna try and help you, okay?"

Thad nodded, glanced at Royal, and then locked eyes with Hick, a glimmer of hope on his face.

Hick turned back to Carol. "Okay?"

She sighed and looked around the shack again. "Okay, let's go."

∾

Dewey opened the door to the darkness and noise outside. Hick noted that between the shed and Royal's car, there was a line at the back door of the barn where customers came from far and wide to purchase Willie's moonshine. In front of the barn people laughed and drank around several bonfires. Wagers were made on cockfighting and boxing, and money changed hands. Loud music came from a tiny pavilion and couples were dancing. It was a raucous crowd and there were plenty of people out in the yard cavorting under the moonlight. Getting Carol Quinn to Royal's car would not be an issue. She was just a young woman, somewhat out of place, but by no means the only female present. But Willie did not sell to colored folks and would not have them on the premises. If seen, Thad's presence would raise some eyebrows. Earl Brewster might not come around, but Hoyt Smith and plenty of others would tell him what they saw.

Hick, Adam, and Royal were discussing what to do when Dewey shook his head. "Son of a bitch. Ya'll sure make things harder than they have to be." With that, he grabbed Thad and threw him over his shoulder like a cotton sack. "Go ahead and make a ruckus, kid."

With that, Thad began to squirm and shout, "Put me down!" as Dewey walked from the shack toward the dirt road.

The lawmen stood, dumbfounded and heard a voice in the darkness call, "What you got there, Dewey?"

"Just another damned kid trying to get at the moonshine," he said, carrying the still hollering Thad out toward the road.

Royal grinned. "Hellfire and tarnation! I sure admire the way Dewey handled that."

Adam took Carol's arm and led her out of the shack through the yard leaving Hick and Royal behind. They followed Adam and made their way across the yard when Royal stopped. "What the hell?" he muttered and stalked toward a young woman sitting alone on a log beside a campfire.

"Patsy!" Royal said in a sharp voice, causing the girl to jump. "What are you doing out here?"

Her eyes widened when she saw Royal and she hopped from the log saying, "Oh Royal! Please don't tell my daddy!"

"You should be switched for being out here! This ain't no place for a good girl."

"I know that," she said. "It's just so many of my friends are here. But ... those poor roosters." She shook her head. "There was so much blood ..." Her eyes trailed toward the barn, with its riotous laughter.

"Billy bring you out here?" Royal asked in a clipped, tense voice.

"No. He's at home studying to re-take his geometry test."

"Then why are you here?"

"A bunch of the kids were coming, and I just wanted to see it for myself. It seemed like a good night because none of us has homework and Billy's busy."

Royal removed his hat and ran his hand across the back of his neck. "Why, Patsy? Why would you want to see a place like this?"

She looked at her hands. "Everyone's been talking about it." She shook her head. "But it ain't no place for me. I shouldn't have come."

"You want a ride home?"

She glanced toward the barn once more. "I need to tell my friends."

"They don't seem overly worried about you right now."

Patsy rose. "Just let me tell them, and then I want to go home. They'll think I'm a square, but it doesn't matter. I don't want to be here anymore."

Hick watched as Patsy made her way toward a group of teenagers at the barn. They paused in their laughter when she approached and then turned back to the spectacle in the barn as she walked away.

"I'm ready," she said to Royal. "Only promise me you won't tell my daddy."

Royal rolled his eyes. "I promise. But next time I catch you at a place like this, he'll hear about it." Royal marched the girl toward his squad car.

"There won't be a next time, I swear. Thank you, Royal," she said as they approached the car. Carol and Thad were already inside and Adam was waiting outside.

"Where's Dewey?" Royal asked.

"He said he had work to do," Adam replied.

"Who is—" Patsy began, when Royal cut her off.

"I don't say a word, you don't say a word. Deal?"

She nodded. "Deal."

Adam climbed into the back seat with Carol and Thad while Royal, Hick, and Patsy got into the front.

The drive was made in a tense silence, the girl wringing her hands, and Royal's jaw clenched. Hick let his curiosity simmer until the squad car stopped in front of a nice, well-maintained home. Hick stepped out of the car to let the girl out.

"Thank you," she said to Royal, her voice breathless with relief.

"Patsy, I ain't never in my life ever thought I'd see a preacher's daughter down there at that juke joint," Royal said walking around the car and looking at her with obvious disapproval.

Tears formed in her eyes. "You won't find me there again, I promise. I ain't ever going back."

Royal's face was rigid with anger—and sorrow. He shook his head and looked away. "I wish I could believe that, but you done got in with the wrong crowd. Those boys are all a bunch of rounders, and your friend Billy wants to be just like them. Only reason he ain't is 'cause of his daddy. I told you before you need to stay away from those kids, but you won't listen to reason, and I'm done talking." He turned back and his voice was cold and tense. "Don't forget," he said, "we made a deal."

"I won't forget," she said and walked up the sidewalk toward the house. She paused on the front porch and turned back, managing a small smile before she went inside.

"You want to tell me what that was about?" Hick asked Royal as they climbed back into the car.

Royal slammed the car in gear and headed toward the Catholic Church. "Just a girl I used to know."

"Your friend Willie make it a habit of selling hooch to kids?"

Royal shrugged. "Not to my knowledge. But then again, Willie ain't always forthcoming with his activities."

Royal stopped at the four way intersection and then motored through it and into the parking lot of the church where Adam's car was parked. The lights in the church were still on and Hick told Adam, "Get them in your car. I'm going to run in and tell the preacher we got Thad so Enos can quit fretting."

Adam nodded and hurriedly ushered Carol and Thad into his car while Hick went into the church. Father Grant was pacing the floor, and when he saw Hick, relief flooded his face.

"You find Thad?"

"I did," Hick told him.

The door to Father Grant's office opened and Esther, Thad's sister, along with an older woman stepped out.

"This is Ida Burton," Father Grant said. "Thad's mother."

Ida crossed the room and took Hick's hands into hers. "You take care of my boy. He's a good son. He helps out his daddy when he can and he never caused me one bit of trouble." She paused. "He's my little angel." A calm, dignified strength showed in her eyes. "I don't know what you can do for us, but keep him safe. That's all I ask."

"I'll do my best," Hick promised. "I'm taking him and that lawyer back to Cherokee Crossing. I think they'll be safer there. You think Enos will be okay with that?"

"Enos will not be okay with that," Ida Burton said with a voice that commanded respect. "But I will."

14

Tuesday, July 20, 1954

The darkness of a dreamless sleep was broken by the feeling of a presence hovering near. Startled from this half-sleep, Hick felt an arm brush across him and came to complete wakefulness, instinctively grabbing a nearby wrist and opening his eyes at the same time.

"Jesus Christ, Hillbilly," said Carol Quinn in a shocked voice. "I was just getting a cigarette."

Hick shook his head, blinked the sleep from his eyes, and released the wrist. Carol rubbed it with her other hand and regarded him strangely. "Jumpy, aren't you?"

"I'm sorry." Hick rubbed his eyes.

"I thought you were awake."

Hick rubbed his stiff neck and stretched his head backward, grimacing in pain. He coughed and said, "I am now. What time is it?"

"Almost seven."

"Here," Hick said, handing her the cigarette pack and lighter. "I hope I didn't hurt you."

Carol shook her head. "Just startled me. I didn't expect you to lash out like that."

"Yeah, well, like I said, I'm sorry. You get any sleep?"

"Not a wink. You?"

Hick shook his head. "I never sleep much here."

"You stay here often?" She glanced around the room.

"Every other night." Hick rose and moved to the doorway looking in on Thad who snored peacefully on a cot. "Wonder what will happen to him."

Carol joined Hick in the doorway. "He's a good kid," she said. "Before they locked us up in that shed I had a few choice things to say about you, that kid deputy Adkins, and everyone else who lives south of the Mason Dixon line. He told me I shouldn't be too hard on folks. Said they're just doing the best they can." She shook her head. "He's a hell of a lot more gracious than me."

"So tell me … what's your plan?" Hick asked.

She raised her eyebrows.

"You do have a plan, don't you? You are a lawyer."

She took a long draw from the cigarette, leaned against the doorway, and closed her eyes. "I can't actually practice down here, and I sure as hell didn't have a clue what I was getting into."

"Well, what did you—" Hick began and then stopped. "Why don't you start from the beginning? Exactly why did you come here?"

Carol took another drag and stared at the tip a moment. "I don't know. I guess I was desperate."

"What does that mean?"

"Desperate. To stand out. To make a name for myself." Hick handed her an ashtray and she nodded her thanks. "The phone call started everything. It came in to the firm late Friday evening. After the men had already left for their club." Her eyes hardened and met Hick's. "They don't have to work quite as hard as I do."

"I see," Hick said.

"No, you don't. You don't see anything. You don't see me busting my ass and coming in the top three percent of my class only to be hired as a legal secretary. I passed the bar, and for what? To get the guys coffee?" She rolled her eyes. "I didn't go to law school to clerk or to bring someone their coffee. I went to be a lawyer. But women lawyers … no one takes us seriously."

She walked to the window and looked outside. "When I applied for my job, you know what they said? 'You have an impressive record Miss Quinn, but a pretty girl like you will likely marry. You must see our position. Why we can't really give you any important cases." She stabbed the cigarette out in the ashtray. "My big brother went to law school and it took him three times to pass the bar. Three times! I passed on my first try. But he's a Defense Attorney in New York." She sighed. "All I am is the coffee girl."

"If that's the case, why'd your firm send you down here?"

"No one sent me down here. I volunteered. My firm in New York is watching very closely what is happening in the south. For years, Negroes up north have fought in the courts and finally are beginning to win some important cases, but down here … colored folks haven't had much luck. My firm sat by and watched several cases to go the Supreme Court, one ending in a landmark decision. It didn't take long for them to realize they had missed a golden opportunity and they're making up for lost time. Cases in places like Chicago and St. Louis were just the beginning. The rumbling is beginning down here and where money and prestige are at stake, my firm can sound convincing ... at times even I believe they care. They think civil rights will begin to explode across the south, and they're trying to make their presence felt ... they want in on it. Hell, in February they even got quoted in *LOOK* magazine regarding school desegregation in Phoenix."

She crossed the room and looked in on the sleeping boy. She shook her head, and snorted softly. "But, when I told them about this kid ..." She shrugged her shoulders and in a whisper continued, "No one cares about this place ... or Thad. He's just a young black kid in trouble in a small town. He's got no money, there's nothing unique or important here, so there's no way in hell one of those bastards would give him a minute of their time." She shrugged. "I talked to my brother, and he said any experience is better than none so I begged for the opportunity to come down here and advise."

"What can you do?"

She glanced up quickly. "Do? I hardly know where to begin. The caller never mentioned corruption or danger. Just that a young, colored boy had been unjustly accused of a crime and might be ignorant of his rights. Said there was no local lawyer he'd trust to advise the kid. My opportunities to actually do something besides clerk are so few and far between … anyway my brother said this would get me some credibility." Her eyes traveled around the police station. "But this … I never envisioned this."

"And who the hell is this mystery caller?" Hick asked, running his hand through his hair.

"I have no idea."

The door to the station opened and Adam entered carrying a thermos and picnic basket. "I see you're up. Pam sent some coffee and breakfast."

"Thanks." Hick took the thermos from Adam, poured a cup of coffee, handed it to Carol and, then poured one for himself. After taking a drink he asked, "You see Harrington already?"

Adam nodded. "I saw Harrington, Coleman, and Pringle. Those bastards, whoever they are, have been all over town handing out those flyers."

"What flyers?" Carol asked.

"There's a political rally over in Broken Creek next Wednesday for Senator John Richardson. He's running for governor and the primary is July 27," Hick explained.

Thad stirred in his sleep and they heard him yawn loudly.

"What do you aim we do about him?" Adam asked. "We can't hide these two here forever."

Hick glanced toward Thad. "The way I see it, we're going to have to figure out who was driving that truck. The only thing we know is who wasn't."

"Sounds like a tall order," Adam said.

"It is," Hick agreed.

Adam walked to the doorway and looked in on Thad. Turning, he said, "What happens if we don't?"

Hick sighed and then looked from Carol to Adam. Sadness welled in him. "If we don't, Thad's going to have to plead guilty."

"What?" Carol cried.

Hick drew Adam and Carol away from Thad's hearing. "Brewster's brother is the coroner," he whispered. "The judge is his cousin. Hell, he's even distantly related to Senator Richardson. His mama is related by marriage to the Attorney General. I'm telling you Thad's got about a snowball's chance in hell of getting a fair trial. I've been up all night going over this and unless we can prove corruption, unless we can find out who really did this and why Brewster's covering for them, Thad's best option is to plead guilty. Six years in a juvenile camp is better than life in prison … or worse."

"I can't believe that's his best option," Carol said, shaking her head.

The phone rang, and Adam went to his desk to answer it.

"Brewster has been trouble down here for years. When you have a man with no scruples connected to power, it just stands to reason that he will always work for what's in his own best interest. He aims to get this case closed fast and put Thad away."

"But why?" Carol began, when Adam called them to the front of the station.

Adam's face was tense. "That was the preacher, Grant. Apparently Broken Creek had a rough night. The Missionary

Baptist Church was burned to the ground, and some kids have been driving around the colored side of town shooting guns."

"Why all the violence?" Carol asked.

"Hell if I know," Hick said. "They ain't ever had this kind of trouble in Broken Creek."

"And Grant says Enos wants his boy back. Now."

Carol bit her lip. "My firm in New York may be more interested in this case than I thought. This is more than just me advising a kid ignorant of his legal rights. It sounds like the town is getting really worked up about something and helping a poor, colored child in the face of a bigoted, angry mob is just the kind of publicity they're looking for. They might send one of their hotshot attorneys down here to advise after all."

"But this was your chance," Hick argued.

"I've never tried a case, not even a preliminary hearing, so my expertise is limited. If I can convince them to send someone more experienced it will help Thad." Carol's eyes narrowed. "The trouble is, when that damned deputy snatched me from my motel room, I grabbed my purse, but he didn't give me time to get my briefcase. The arrest warrant, the coroner's report, and the witness statement from the man whose truck was stolen all are in there. My firm will need this information before they decide if they'll send someone to help. If this isn't special enough, if there isn't something unique and important going on here, they won't waste their time. I'm going to have to talk fast and do a lot of convincing. I don't have a minute to spare if that judge is due back tomorrow. Someone has to be on a plane today, and they need to know what they're up against."

She looked at Hick and Adam with a determined face. "I need my briefcase."

"Getting back to your motel room in Broken Creek could be tough," Adam answered, his eyes dark with anger. "Grant says Brewster's looking high and low for Thad. He thinks he's headed our way."

15

July 20, 1954

Hick tripped over a wagon in the yard and cursed silently as he rushed from the car into the house. Maggie and Mourning both stopped what they were doing and stood in stunned silence as he burst through the door.

"Hickory!" Maggie exclaimed, her face white with shock. "What's happened?"

He crossed the room and took her arm, looking into her face. "Mag, I'm taking you, Mourning, and the boys to go and stay with Pam."

"But—"

"Just listen to me," he said, his voice tense. "Brewster's on the war path and I don't want him coming here and finding you alone."

"I don't understand. Why would he come here?"

"We've got that little colored boy here—in Cherokee. And I think Brewster knows it. Or at least suspects it. I'm not sure what he'll do or where he'll go, but he could be headed this way."

"Be reasonable. Earl Brewster won't—"

Hick interrupted again. "Earl Brewster is desperate and feeling threatened. He's mad as hell, and I don't want you here by yourself. Especially in your condition. Please, Mag, just do this for me."

Maggie studied her husband's face. "My God … What do you think he will do?"

"He won't do anything because he's a coward and we both know that. But like most cowards he's got a big mouth and he'll bluster and fuss and act tough. I don't want you around him alone." He closed his eyes. "I should have never gotten involved."

She pulled back and shook her head. "You know you couldn't live with yourself if you hadn't. You couldn't sit back and watch a child's life be thrown away."

Her words unintentionally stabbed him and his breath caught in his lungs. His mind reeled back in time as he recalled another child, this one in a freezing, farmhouse in Belgium. Tears smarted behind his eyes, and he cleared his throat.

"I'll drop you off at Pam's house," he said. "I'm meeting Adam and that lawyer there. I need to get her back to Broken Creek so she can get some papers that are in her briefcase to help Thad. How long before—"

"We're ready," Mourning said, holding up a satchel filled with extra clothes and toys for the boys.

"Thanks, Mourning."

He hesitated and then walked to the bedroom. He pulled a box from the top shelf of the closet. He opened it and picked up the pistol, the one, as sheriff, he was supposed to carry.

Feeling Maggie behind him, he turned and met her questioning glance. His sons peered from behind her, wide-eyed and too young to understand, but sensing something was wrong.

"Daddy?" Jimmy said, coming forward and looking up.

Hick looked at the pistol and then put it back. He knelt and encircled his boys within his arms. A small voice within him spoke accusingly, telling him he had placed his family in danger.

As if reading his thoughts, Maggie whispered, "This ain't your doing. This is Earl Brewster's doing."

He hugged his children and then rose. "Let's get to Pam's. The sooner I get on the road to Broken Creek, the sooner I'll be back."

Hick drove his family to Adam and Pam's house where Adam was waiting, with Thad Burton and Carol Quinn in tow.

"I called Doc," Adam said, striding out to Hick, his face tense. "He's on his way out here, just in case Brewster takes it in his mind to look here for Thad. I'll be the 'welcoming committee' at the station."

Hick nodded, glancing at the house. "Thanks. Is Carol ready?"

"Yeah. She'll be right out."

Mourning took Thad and the boys inside, but Maggie lingered. "Hickory," she said in a voice full of emotion, "be careful."

He put his arms around her and kissed her, wanting to stay, wanting to protect her, wanting to be protected by her love and strength. He felt her breath on his cheek, and closed his eyes for a moment. Then he pulled away. "I'll be back soon. I promise."

He turned to Adam. "Does Pam know what to do if Brewster shows up?"

"She'll put Thad in the root cellar if needed. I don't think Brewster would have the guts to barge into a Deputy Sheriff's house without a warrant no matter how desperate he is."

"If he's headed this way, I reckon Brewster will be here in Cherokee Crossing in about a half hour," Hick said, glancing at the sun.

Adam's eyes shone with excitement. "I'll be sure and make him feel at home."

Hick turned to Maggie. "I know it's hot, but make sure the kids stay inside."

She nodded and Hick turned to Adam, "You'll check back here in a half hour to make sure everyone's okay?"

"You bet your ass. I'll be back every five minutes if I think I need to. I dare that son of a bitch to say or do anything. By the time I'm through with him, he'll wish to hell he'd stayed in Broken Creek."

The only thing on earth that could ever provoke the usually good-natured Adam to violence was threatening his family. Hick pitied Brewster if he took it in his head to show up at the Kinion house unannounced.

"I'm thinking if we take the back roads back toward Broken Creek and Brewster is on the way here we should miss him." He glanced at his watch. "Will you stay here until Doc arrives?"

Adam nodded.

"I'll call as soon as we get to the motel." Hick said. He turned once more to Maggie. "I'll see you soon." He kissed her forehead and turned away. "Ready?" he asked Carol who was making her way down the porch steps.

She nodded and they climbed into Hick's car. He glanced back one last time at Maggie. The sun flared into the rear-view mirror and then she was gone.

"You have a lovely family," Carol said as the car pulled onto a dirt road.

"Thanks."

"And you really think they could be in danger?"

Hick shrugged. "Probably not. But this pregnancy has been hard on my wife. I don't want her dealing with Earl Brewster, especially when he's angry and desperate. And with everything that went on last night in Broken Creek—"

They drove in silence for a moment and then Carol asked, "Why is this Brewster so intent on putting Thad away?"

"I'm not sure." Hick answered, lighting a cigarette.

Carol picked through her purse and then asked, "Can I have one of those? I'm out."

Hick handed her a cigarette and his lighter and she took a long drag. "My God, it's flat here," she said, staring out the window and then handing him back the lighter.

Hick glanced out the window at the rows of cotton, green stripes flying past the car windows, broken up only by the occasional tree break.

"So, why the fire and gunshots in Broken Creek last night? What has everyone so upset? It's not Thad, is it?"

"No. It has nothing to do with Thad."

"What flyers were you talking about?"

Hick reached into his shirt pocket and handed her the flyer that Benji and Jack brought from the cotton field. "These have been going around Cherokee Crossing. I expect Broken Creek has seen their fair share, too."

Carol skimmed it quickly and then turned her eyes to Hick. "So, this Richardson is running on a segregationist platform?"

Hick nodded. "And Broken Creek is the perfect venue. They were set to desegregate the schools next year but suddenly got cold feet."

Carol read through the flyer again. "I've never heard of Citizens Against Desegregation. This must be another one."

"Another one?"

"These groups are springing up all over the south. The White Rights Movement, Concerned White Americans. They like to distance themselves from other groups like the Klan, pretending they're not about hate and violence. But when you single out a vulnerable population and convince people that this group is somehow inferior and trying to take something away from you, you instill fear and that breeds anger and that breeds violence. These groups may be wrapped up in flowery language and they may have some mighty important advocates, governors and senators to name just a few, but at their heart, they're just the Klan all over again."

"And violence is exactly what they've incited."

"So what happens to Thad?"

"Enos Burton is right to be worried about his boy. The town's so riled against colored folks right now that they can't stand the thought that Thad might get away with something. Especially since the victim was a white man. I'm sure this is working in Brewster's favor, and it's not hurting Richardson's message either. Right now Enos has gotta be scared to death for his son."

"But Thad has nothing to do with any of this. Why pick on a kid?"

"He's colored. For Brewster, that's enough." Hick threw his cigarette out the window.

Nodding, Carol took another long drag of the cigarette and stared at the scenery going by. After a moment she said, "I thought this was just a lazy sheriff trying to wrap up a case with as little work as possible. There's more going on here than I imagined. A lot more." She leaned forward and put her cigarette out in the car's ashtray. "To hell with my law firm. I know someone else who'll be interested in this."

"Who?"

"My uncle. He works for the Department of Justice."

"Why would the Department of Justice care about any of this?"

"Oh, a lot of reasons. First, I suspect we're dealing with 'color of law' violations."

Hick looked over at her. "What does that mean?"

"When you perform your duties as a legal representative of the county, those duties are done within the color of law.

When you misuse your authority, you violate the color of law and that is a serious offense, one the FBI takes great interest in. I thought I was coming down here to bail a kid out of jail and explain to him that he had the right to an attorney and representation. I thought the root problems in Broken Creek were ignorance and laziness, not corruption. The truth of the matter is, this is more than a bad arrest. Brewster knowingly arrested and imprisoned Thad on false evidence. You can't arrest someone and hold them over without bond the way he did and call it 'safekeeping'. He misused his authority to take advantage of Thad."

"He's done that and more. We've had someone go missing that I think could be connected—a witness, or maybe even the perpetrator.

"That's what you meant when you said one person was already missing, back when we were in that shack."

"Yeah. I didn't want to say more and scare Thad. Also you should know Brewster went out of his way to make sure Thad's fingerprints would be in that truck."

"These are serious charges. If we can prove them that will be nail number one in the fat bastard's coffin. Brewster could go to prison for life," Carol said.

Hick shook his head. "I don't like it. He's gonna get desperate."

"You're right," Carol said. "And color of law violations could be the least of his problems. If he's involved with the Citizens Against Desegregation and they're the ones inciting violence ..." She shook her head. "The Supreme Court has ruled and desegregation is the law of the land.

My Uncle Arthur works for the Civil Rights Section of the Department of Justice. Eisenhower doesn't want them to get involved, but I believe Uncle Arthur could get a couple of J. Edgar Hoover's boys down here to looks things over."

"I'd welcome any help," Hick said. "I'm not exactly sure what we're dealing with, but I know it's more than I'm used to."

Carol looked at him a moment and then said, "Well, Hillbilly, that's more than a lot of men would admit. Usually law enforcement agencies object to working together."

"This is not about me or my reputation. This is about Thad." He shot her a grim, but determined smile. "Like you, I'd welcome anything that could help him."

She held his gaze and nodded. "Uncle Arthur's the one we need down here."

It was still morning when they arrived in Broken Creek, but already the harsh sun made the humid air stifling. "I want to run in real quick and talk to Father Grant. I need to let him know what we're doing so he can tell Thad's daddy." Hick turned the car toward the church. "And you're sure your uncle will send down some help?"

"Police corruption is one of the Justice Department's specialties. Once I let them know what's going on here, Brewster's going to find himself in a lot of trouble. You can get away with plenty in small town America because it's easy to operate with impunity in the sticks." She eyed Hick, but he said nothing. "But once word gets out, once someone hears about it—"

"We still need to find out who really killed that vagrant last week," Hick said. "There's a reason Brewster was in such a hurry to wrap this up. Somebody in this town is carrying a hell of a secret. There has to be a way to get them to talk."

He stepped from the car and was making his way to the church when he felt something sharp press into his back. "Don't turn around," a voice hissed in his ear.

"What do you want?" Hick heard Carol ask and he started to turn his head when the sharp object pricked at him again, hard enough where he felt the point break the skin.

"I said don't turn around," the speaker said again. "My friend ain't gonna hurt that lady. We don't aim to hurt either of you." The voice took on a begging sound. "Please don't make a scene. We just need to go for a walk."

"Where are we going?" Hick asked as the knife prodded him toward the nearby cotton field.

"You'll know when we get there."

16

Tuesday, July 20, 2016

Grasshoppers and praying mantises buzzed through the high, but thin cotton. Hick's shirt stuck to his back as he walked through the tall plants, the sound of stumbling steps assuring him that Carol was close behind. "You work for Brewster?" he said, trying to turn to see the man behind him.

A snort followed the comment and the knife prodded him forward again.

The cotton plants seemed to hug the humidity, pulling it down upon Hick. Sweat streamed down his back and dripped beneath his hat, stinging his eyes. He heard Carol stumble and a voice say, "Ma'am, you might want to take them shoes off. They ain't exactly made for comfort."

"Yes, you're right," she said, her voice breathless from the brisk walk. They paused in their steps and a moment later, Hick heard her say, "Thank you."

"We're almost there, ma'am," the other man's voice said as if trying to reassure Carol. Hick wondered if there was a knife at her back, too

Again, by instinct, Hick began to turn and, again, the knife pierced his skin. "Ain't no need for you to look," his captor whispered near his ear. "We all gonna be fine as long as you keep walking."

Hick detected a fearful plea in this command, but simply nodded and continued blindly through the high cotton. In the distance he spied the outline of a large, abandoned cotton gin. Their steps brought them nearer and finally, the long rows of cotton were behind them and they were in the open, which felt cool in spite of the sweltering July heat.

"Stop right here," the voice behind Hick ordered.

"What's this all about?"

"You'll see."

Hick waited and moments later Enos Burton came out of the cotton gin.

"Enos? What's going on?"

"Go on boys," Enos said, nodding to the men who had brought Hick and Carol. Hick heard their footsteps flee through the cotton fields. "They don't like messin' with a sheriff, and I ain't never raised my hand against the law, but I needed to talk to you someplace where Brewster won't come. I don't want no scene. I just wanted you to walk out here real quiet like. And you did. Don't hold it against them."

"I won't," Hick said. "What's this all about?"

He glanced around. "Come inside."

Hick, Carol, and Enos walked into the large metal building. It was dark inside, shadows beside patches of startling brightness in places where hail had punched holes through the corrugated tin roof.

"Sit," Enos said, indicating a crate.

Hick sat down and noticed Carol quickly sat beside him. He could feel her trembling and pitied her, but he knew Enos could be trusted.

Enos didn't sit. Instead he paced, as if he didn't quite know what to do with his large hands and massive frame. It was helplessness, something he was clearly unfamiliar with. Finally, he asked, "You ever see a lynching?"

The question startled Hick. So much that he just stared.

Enos shook his head. "I didn't think so. I have. The worst thing about 'em ain't the sound of the muffled screams, the jerking of the legs when the life is torn from the bodies, the stillness of death. It ain't watching your friends swaying from a tree, just a rockin' back and forth in the breeze. No, it ain't none of that. It's the hate that shines in the eyes of them men as they string folks up. It's the darkest, most evil thing I ever seen." He ran his hand over his face, as if trying to block some image.

Hick shifted on the uncomfortable crate and Enos continued. "Sheriff, I know you want to help Thad, I really do. But I knowed the first time I laid eyes on you that you don't understand the hate. You ain't seen the hate. You don't know what it's like to be afraid every time your wife or your daughter goes to the store, that she ain't gonna come back because some white boy might take it in his mind he'd like to try some of that."

Enos walked to the door of the gin and stared out across

the cotton. "My boy, Thad, is a good kid. He ain't got a bad bone in his body." He turned and looked at Hick and Carol. "That's all my wife's doing. He was born when I was in the Philippines. I didn't see him until he was almost three years old."

He shook his head. "I don't know how to make you see, how to explain it, 'cause you can't understand it, no matter how hard you try. You can't understand the hate 'cause you ain't colored. But I understand it, and I fear it." He walked toward Hick. "You got kids?" he asked, unexpectedly.

Hick nodded.

"As one father to another. Please tell me where my boy is. Please help me get him back in that jail. I know he didn't do what Brewster said he done. Everybody know that. But sometimes you just gotta take it. You gotta take it 'cause there ain't no other way."

Hick looked into Enos' eyes. The man was begging for his son's life.

Enos eyes closed and his lips began to tremble. "I don't ever want anyone to look at my son with that kind of hate. He ain't capable of understanding it. The day will come when he will, but, Lord Jesus, not yet. Let him be my baby just a little bit longer." Enos covered his face with his large hand. "He's the only boy I have."

Hick recalled the hope that shone from Thad's eyes. It had been unfair, cruel really, to raise such a hope in a child—a hope that could not flourish in an ugly world. Something inside Hick broke and his heart ached with sadness. "Thad's at my sister's house in Cherokee Crossing," he finally said.

He heard Carol gasp, but continued, "We hid him away because we think Brewster's gone there to look for him."

"I'm gonna go get him and bring him back to that jail," Enos said, moving toward the doorway. "They won't touch him there. I want my boy safe from all that's been going on around here."

Hick nodded. "My sister lives on Third Street, on the outskirts of town. If you go to the police station my Deputy, Adam, can you take you there. They got a houseful of boys. Adam'll understand. You can trust him." He paused. "You sure about this?"

"I'm sure," Enos said, his voice full of bitter resignation.

"Okay," Hick said. "I've still got a day to figure this out before the Judge gets here. I'll do my best."

Enos was already heading out the door, but he paused and turned. "I know. But sometimes our best just ain't good enough."

17

Tuesday, July 20, 1954

"Why the hell did you tell him?" Carol demanded as they marched back through the cotton.

Hick turned and watched her struggle through the sandy soil, her arms swinging wildly. "I've got no right to keep Enos from his son."

"So that's it? Thad's back in jail and you're okay with this?"

Hick's pulse quickened and his eyes flashed. "No! I am not okay with it," he snapped. "But it's probably the safest bet for Thad until we get this sorted out. What if he's at my sister's and Brewster finds out and brings a mob? What if they yank Thad out of there in front of my wife and kids? I've seen what anger and hate do to people."

He shook his head and his mouth set in a grim line. "The truth of the matter is, we may not be able to help Thad because people can be blind to the truth when they don't like what they see. You don't like it and I don't like it, but we have to face facts."

He stalked forward and after a moment he heard Carol's sliding footsteps follow.

The car waited in the parking lot, the bright sunshine gleamed off the windshield and he opened both of the doors and cranked down the windows.

"Those seats will be hot as fire," he explained. "We'll let it air out a minute."

"Okay," Carol answered, pouring sandy dirt from a high heeled pump before putting her shoe back on. "My nylons are ruined," she said, with a shake of her head.

Hick leaned against the car and lit two cigarettes, handing one to Carol.

"Well, Hillbilly, you sure know how to keep a lady entertained," she said, taking the cigarette. "What time is it?"

Hick glanced at his watch. "A little past eleven."

She shrugged. "So what's next? Do I even bother calling anyone? There aren't that many flights into Memphis. Our window of opportunity is closing."

"I don't …" Hick began.

The door of the church opened and a clearly relieved Father Grant walked to them. "I noticed your car was here about a half hour ago but I couldn't, for the life of me, think of where you might have gone. I'm glad to see you're okay."

"We're fine," Hick said. "Just had a talk with Enos. He's headed to Cherokee Crossing to fetch Thad and hand him back over to Brewster. He's scared."

"I'm not surprised," Father Grant said with a frown. "After last night, I had a feeling that might happen."

"What exactly went on here last night?" Hick asked.

"Let me show you," Grant said, walking toward the church. Hick followed and Grant said, "See this? A bullet hole. There are about six of these in my church, but at least it's still standing. The Baptist Church down the road wasn't so lucky. And the churches aren't the only things on the colored side of town to be riddled with bullet holes. It's a miracle no one was killed."

"Cowards," Carol spat.

The two men turned and Hick said, "I'm sorry. This is Carol Quinn, the lawyer from New York. And this is Father Grant. Thad's sister works for him."

"How do you do?" Father Grant said.

Carol shook his hand. "A little shaken, but uninjured."

"That would be a fitting description for Broken Creek, Arkansas," he replied. "I've been at this parish for over seven years and this town has always been a peaceful place. The whites and the coloreds may not worship together or socialize, but they live together, work together, shop together, they've always been on friendly terms. I keep telling myself that it was only a few—just a bunch of stupid kids out having what they thought was a 'good time' because they're feeling bold right now. But where was our sheriff? Where is the outcry from Broken Creek over what happened here? It's like the whole town collectively shut their doors and turned out the lights."

Hick took the flyer from his pocket and handed it to Grant, asking, "You see any of these around?"

Grant nodded. "This rally is the talk of the town. Senator John Richardson is the keynote speaker. He's trying to nab the Democratic nomination for governor and segregation will be the cornerstone of his campaign." His mouth curled in a bitter smirk. "There was a time Richardson was supportive of desegregation, but he's got some skeletons in his closet. The specter of communism has been raised and he's got to distance himself from any kind of progressive thought. His best chance for election is to exploit and exaggerate. And he's not stupid. He knows if he gives people something to feel passionate about, he'll have a better chance of the right ones showing up at the polls."

"And those people will do their damndest to see the wrong ones don't," Carol added.

"I'm afraid you're right," Grant agreed. "The south is not going to give up segregation without a fight. It's a way of life." A bewildered look crossed his face and he looked off into the distance. "The funny thing is, if you question most southerners you'll find they don't hate colored people. In fact, they like their neighbors. The average person doesn't take the time to sit down and think about what segregation really means ... that somehow someone is less of a man because of the color of his skin, that they're entitled to less, that they aren't fully human. They don't understand it because they've never experienced it and it's just the way it's always been." He shook his head. "With this kind of lazy intellect, people will never understand the evil they are promulgating. They'll make one excuse and then another ... there's always an excuse."

"But, I don't get it," Hick said. "I thought the Supreme Court settled desegregation. How do you refuse to uphold the law?"

"Senator Richardson's calling down the great god of nullification," Grant said. "He's been all over the state in an effort to get citizens riled against the idea."

"And the ruling was schools must be desegregated with 'all deliberate speed,'" Carol added. "For segregationists that is nothing more than a loophole that means never."

"'Never' won't be an option for long," Grant said. "Once the wheels of progress begin turning there's no stopping them. Richardson can get people riled up, but he knows there's no stopping desegregation. He's using ignorance to gain power and my guess is his presence here will keep pressure on our school board so they don't weaken in their new-found resolve to keep the schools separate."

"What do you make of this new-found resolve?" Hick asked.

"I don't know what to think," Grant said, with a shake of his head. "Ike Davis had convinced the board to agree with him, saying desegregating the school was not only economically advantageous, it was morally right. He was the one who drove the idea forward and then he was the one who convinced them to wait. I wonder if he got a whiff of all this coming down and thought it might endanger the students or be too disruptive to their education."

"He's the one I ran into here the other night," Hick said.

"Yeah. President of the School Board. It was at his urging that desegregating the Broken Creek schools came up in the first place."

"Is this Davis easily manipulated or intimidated?" Hick asked.

"Ike was in the trenches in World War One. He's seen everything and is not easily moved. That's why his change of heart took me by surprise. He was a staunch ally and he seemed to change almost overnight."

Hick thought for a moment. "This Davis, when he came to see you … did he have any bruises on his face, any injuries you could see?"

"No," Grant answered. "There was nothing wrong with him. Why?"

Hick glanced across the cotton field toward the old cotton gin and sighed. "Well all of this—the racial unrest, the political nonsense. It seems to coincide with Thad's trouble. Even if it's not related, it could not have come at a worse time for him. We're running out of time, and I don't know what to do."

Grant unbuttoned the top button of his shirt and loosened his white collar. "Brewster has to be stopped. Thad isn't the first kid he's dragged into court without just cause, and he won't be the last."

"We all know what could happen if this goes to trial," Hick said with a frown.

"Yes," Grant said. "But I also know that the truth has a way of making itself known. Don't forget. Someone out there killed that man and he knows what he did. A guilty conscience is a powerful thing."

"It can also be a quick casualty when it's inconvenient," Hick replied.

Father Grant shook his head. "Don't be so sure. It's one thing to run and hide when you accidentally run over someone in the night. That's nothing more than a natural fear of being caught. But there's more to the heart of man than primal, survival instincts. We each have in us a spark of the divine and it's not easy to snuff out. It can lie dormant, like any spark, but sometimes, it only takes a slight breeze to fan it into flame. It's one thing to make a mistake. It's another thing altogether to sit by and watch an innocent child take the rap."

"I know all about mistakes," Hick said looking down at his shoes. "But I also believe that there are plenty of people who will gladly keep their mouth shut to save their own skin."

"Perhaps," Grant conceded. "But, we weren't created to live that way. There's something in the heart of man that craves justice and order. I believe the person who killed that man is suffering. There's only so much we can take before guilt begins to tear us apart. Every day that still, small voice will grow louder and louder."

"Unfortunately, we are out of days. We only have twenty-four hours, and I don't see anyone stepping up to confess before the judge returns tomorrow." He turned to Carol. "What do you want to do? This could be dangerous."

Carol tossed the cigarette to the ground and stepped on it. "The quicker I make this call the quicker we'll get help." She looked into his face. "We need to stop this fat bastard."

"Then, I guess we're going." They climbed into the car and Hick told Grant, "Miss Quinn's got a phone call to make so we're headed to the motel. We want to get in and out real quick and then back to Cherokee Crossing. If things get out of hand and you need help call Adkins. If you can't get him, call Adam in Cherokee. We plan on being back there in a couple of hours."

Grant put his hands on the car door and leaned in. "Folks get word what you're trying to do and who you're trying to help and there could be trouble for you. Be careful."

"Thanks," Hick said. He started the car and put it into gear. "We will."

18
Tuesday, July 20, 1954

"Everything's fine," Hick told Adam on the phone. "We're at the hotel now and as soon as Miss Quinn makes her phone call, we're leaving. She's going through her papers now. Everything okay there?"

"Brewster never showed," Adam's said, his voice tinny over the receiver. "I went by the house and they didn't see him either."

"Maggie and the boys okay?"

"Maggie was lying down and the boys were eating cheese sandwiches."

Hick smiled. "I'm glad she's resting." Carol waved the papers in front of Hick impatiently and he said, "Will you tell her I called? Tell her I'm okay? Carol needs the phone so I have to hang up now."

"I'll let her know," Adam said. "It'll take some worry off her mind."

"Thanks, Adam," Hick said. "For everything."

"Hurry back."

"I will," Hick said into the phone before hanging up.

"It's already 12:30 in Washington," Carol said taking the receiver from Hick and biting her lip. "Uncle Arthur may be at lunch." She was facing the door and had begun to dial when her eyes fixated on something behind Hick. The color drained from her cheeks.

"Well, look who finally came home," a voice Hick recognized as Earl Brewster's said.

Spinning around, Hick saw Sheriff Brewster and a jittery Royal Adkins enter the room.

Brewster's face was red with anger. "I have been all over this green earth looking for you. I want to know where the hell Thad Burton is. He's supposed to be at home and no place else, and I'm done playing games! You sons of bitches have messed with my plans long enough." Brewster crossed the room and grabbed Carol by the wrist, twisting the phone from her grasp. "Who the hell are you calling, little lady?"

"I have to check in with my office in New York. It's Tuesday. If I don't call they'll know something's wrong. They'll send people here to look for me."

Brewster seemed to be considering what she said. After a moment, he said, "Make the call." Hick moved toward Brewster who pulled his pistol from the holster. Pointing it at Hick's head, Brewster said, "Only watch what you say or this one will suffer an occupational hazard."

Carol's eyes met Hick's, then she turned back to Brewster and nodded. He handed her the phone.

Hick watched as Carol dialed. After a moment she said, "Yes, ma'am, I'd like to place a long distance call. Yes to New

York. Carol paused and then said, "Yes, ma'am, Foundation 241."

Hick's heart sank at the words 'New York'. Carol would not be able to get the Department of Justice, not with Brewster in the room. No help would be coming.

After giving the number, she waited, seemingly praying as she listened to the ringing.

Finally, Carol said, "Yes, hello." She paused, listening to someone on the other end. "This is Caroline Evelyn Quinn—yes—I'm still in Broken Creek, Arkansas working with that colored boy. This case is much more complex than I anticipated. No, no I don't think I can come back—"

Brewster cleared his throat and cocked the pistol. Carol's eyes widened. "I mean to say, I can do this but I will be delayed. There's an election and that will …" Another pause. "Yes, yes that will work … Okay, thank you." She hung up the phone and looked at Brewster. "Okay?"

Brewster uncocked the pistol. He crossed the room and yanked the phone cord from the wall. "You done real good little lady. Real good." Shaking his head, he said, "Now what am I gonna do with you two?"

"You could send us on our way," Hick said. We've got some things we need to be attending to."

Brewster barked out a nasty laugh. "I'm sure you do. Like warning my prisoner I'm after him. Thad Burton was supposed to stay at home with his daddy, not traipse around the countryside. Now Thad's disappeared right out from under Enos' nose. Looks bad, real bad. Thad's done gone and violated the terms of his release so it's back to jail for him and I'm sure I've got room enough for his negligent daddy, too."

Hick looked at Brewster with disdain. "Enos Burton has done nothing wrong."

Brewster laughed in Hick's face. "As if that matters." He seemed to be considering. "You're gonna have to have an extended stay in Broken Creek. I'm thinking I'll need to stow you away for a day or two." He turned to Royal. "Take the rest of the day off, Dumbass. I won't be needing you."

"But —" Royal began.

"Go on, boy!" Brewster hollered. "You're startin' to really bother me."

Royal's eyes met Hick's, but he left as ordered

Hick watched Royal leave and as soon as the door closed, Brewster moved forward and shoved Hick so hard his neck snapped back and his head banged into the wall.

Brewster's face was red, and he panted from the exertion. "You have been stuck in my craw for years, Blackburn." He stepped closer and growled into Hick's face. "I told you before, you got to learn how to play the game if you're gonna survive."

Hick held his gaze. "The game's changing, Brewster."

"Not my game. Nothing's changing. It's the way of the world. You just never understood your role. Your job is to keep the peace, and it don't matter how you do it. Keep the town folk happy and quiet, that's all you gotta do." He sighed heavily as if trying to help a child understand a difficult concept. "Your predecessor, Sheriff Michaels, understood that. What makes you so different?"

"Maybe because I've seen what hate does to people. When you start using them as scapegoats, when you forget they're human beings, you lose your decency."

Brewster laughed again. "Never had any decency to lose." He narrowed his eyes. "Listen, and listen close, 'cause I'm getting tired of telling you the same story over and over again. I've got a job, and this here is my town. You got no business in Broken Creek and neither does she." He nodded toward Carol. "I can't let you run around and screw up my plans. The Judge will be here tomorrow and all I need is a little hearing. Just a few minutes with Thad saying, 'guilty' when the judge asks him how he pleads. That's all I need … a couple of minutes. Enos Burton knows how the game is played, and he knows what he needs to do. How the hell he lost that kid, I'll never know, but I've got all night to find Thad. And I will."

"And you think we'll just shut up once the judge gets here?" Carol asked.

"You can shut up or talk either one, because it won't matter. The judge is my kin, and unlike you, he knows how things are supposed to work. No, this will be a tidy little hearing. Thad will say he done it, the judge will send Thad away, and the case will be closed." He snapped his fingers. "Hell, maybe Thad will learn a thing or two at that camp that will help him earn a living."

"Who are you protecting? Who really killed that vagrant, Brewster? " Hick asked.

Brewster's mouth gaped open and then snapped shut in an ugly frown. "That kind of talk will get you in a world of hurt. A world of hurt." He leaned heavily into Hick, and put his gun beneath Hick's chin, putting his face close enough that Hick could feel hot breath on his cheek. "I hear tell your wife's having a baby," he said with narrowed eyes. "This is how it's gonna be, you wanna see that kid, you'll walk with me real slow like to the car. You'll keep your mouth shut, and do as you're told. Got it?"

Hick nodded and Brewster grabbed his arm and gave him a shove forward, grinding the pistol into Hick's back. "Open the door and go on out to the car." Turning to Carol, he said, "And you follow."

Hick turned the knob and light from the hot sun overhead stabbed his eyes as he stepped outside. Royal was nowhere to be seen and the motel parking lot was empty of people. Brewster pushed Hick to the car and then reached through the open window for a pair of handcuffs.

He cuffed Hick's hands together in front, opened the back door, and shoved him in. Carol quickly slid beside Hick.

Brewster climbed into the front seat. Hick caught his eyes in the rearview mirror and Brewster said, "You play nice and once this is all cleaned up I'll let you both just walk away. You can go on home to your wife and that little baby. Hell, you might decide you want to be just like me when you see how nice everything turns out."

"I wouldn't count on it," Hick answered. He looked down at his bound hands. "So where to now?"

19

Tuesday, July 20, 1954

"Son of a bitch," Hick grumbled again, glaring at the cuffs. Brewster made a point of finding an extra pair of handcuffs when they arrived at the station and now Carol faced him, both of them handcuffed to a shelving unit in the small, claustrophic storage room. Hick reached into his pocket with his free hand, pulled out two cigarettes, lit them both, and handed one to Carol.

A lone fly buzzed around the room, bouncing against the fluorescent light, trying to find a means of escape. Hick watched it and sympathized. He yanked his left hand again and grimaced as the cuffs dug into his wrist and the metal shelving unit rattled.

From the front of the station came the muffled sounds of Earl Brewster slamming drawers and cursing. Hick leaned his head back and inhaled. Then he stopped and stood up straight. There on a shelf, within easy reach, was the evidence box he and Royal had gone through, the one containing the belongings of Claude Hayes, the hit and run victim.

He closed his eyes and pictured the items inside one by one, then reached over, pulled the box to him, and threw off the lid. He shuffled through the items with his free hand and found the victim's pocket knife. He held it up to Carol.

"We might be able to pick the lock on these cuffs with this. But maybe we should wait till Brewster leaves."

She shook her head. She placed her cigarette on the floor, then reached up to her hair. "This will work better." She showed Hick a bobby pin and then placed the bobby pin in her mouth and bit off the knobbed end.

"Why do I feel like you've done this before?" Hick said with a hint of surprise.

"Because when your favorite uncle works for the Justice Department, you pick up a lot of odd hobbies."

Hick watched as she carefully inserted the bobby pin into the lock on her cuff and began bending it. A phone rang in the front room and they both jumped at the sound.

"Brewster," they heard him say. "What? Where?" A pause. "I'm on it."

Footsteps approached the door and Carol quickly closed her hand over the bobby pin as Hick prayed Brewster wouldn't notice the lidless evidence box. The door opened and Brewster poked his head in. He was wearing a wide smile.

"Someone just phoned in a tip. Might have found my prisoner," he gloated, then laughed. "By tomorrow night, this'll be over." He slowly looked between Hick and Carol, and a slow, sick smile played on his fleshy lips. "All of it will be over." He closed the door and the sound of a key turning in the lock followed. They listened and heard Brewster stomp out of the station and slam the door.

Carol took the bobby pin and again inserted the pin into the handcuff on her right hand and began to turn it when Hick said, "Wait. Start counter-clockwise. It's double locked."

She looked up and nodded. Biting her lip, she maneuvered the bobby pin around. "I wonder who called in that tip."

"I don't know," Hick replied. "Enos probably hasn't even made it to Cherokee Crossing." His eyes moved past the top of Carol's head and, again, spotted the fly, still banging against the fluorescent light. "I wonder if someone in Cherokee called …" he said, letting his voice trail away. He tried to tell himself that Adam had everything under control at home, but there was a nagging worry in the back of his mind that wouldn't go away.

"Damn," Carol said as the bobby pin slipped out of the lock. "I'm not left handed. This will take some doing."

"We're not going anywhere."

"By the way, everything is okay," Carol said, her brow knit in concentration, and not looking up from the lock.

"What do you mean?"

"That call I made."

"You mean the one where you told them you would be here all week insuring that no one will come looking until long after Thad's case is heard?"

"Yeah, that one. Except I didn't call my office."

Hick cocked his head. "Oh?"

"I called Fred. My brother."

"But you told him nothing."

"I told him plenty," she said with a knowing smile. "Growing up, my brother and I made up adventures, invented trouble. Always came to each other's rescue and helped each other escape the bad guys." She shrugged. "We made up a code. If we call each other and use our full names, that means something's wrong. I told you that before I left New York, I told him about this case. He knows where I am. And now he knows I'm in trouble. I mentioned the colored boy and the election. I'm sure he'll call my uncle and Uncle Arthur will send help."

A smile spread across Hick's face. "Well, I'll be damned. Nice work, Miss Quinn."

"Carol," she said. "Please call me Carol." A click sounded from the handcuffs and she raised her eyes and smiled.

"Now turn it clockwise," Hick instructed.

She nodded and went back to work. "Tell me, what was the fat bastard talking about back at the motel?" She looked up at him, her light eyes holding his. Sweat beaded beneath his hairline and he raised his sleeve and mopped his brow. "What did he mean when he said you don't know how the game is played?"

"I guess growing up, I always thought the law did the right thing. Since I became sheriff I've learned that the law has good folks and bad folks, just the same as every other job. And Brewster, well, he's definitely one of the bad ones."

"He sure as hell doesn't like you. Why? Is it because, you don't back him up? You don't condone corruption?"

"Maybe."

She stopped working and regarded him a moment. "I think there's more to you than meets the eye, Hillbilly. When I first saw you I expected you to be the same as all the other cops I've known. I get the job is tough, but so many of them look at anyone other than law enforcement as the enemy. There's nothing wrong with getting at the truth, but they don't like to be questioned. Sometimes they seem to think they're … I don't know, infallible maybe?"

Hick laughed. "Yeah. Well I don't think I'm infallible, that's for damn sure."

A second click sounded and Hick said, "Don't move." He moved beside her and reached down, sliding his fingers down her wrist and lifting the metal strand of the cuff. He maneuvered it open and she slipped the handcuff off and shook her free right hand.

"Now let's get you out of here," she said standing in front of him and inserting the bobby pin into the lock on his handcuff. He tried to avert his eyes because she was so close he felt uncomfortable. He could smell the faint scent of jasmine, could see the muscles in her jaw and neck tighten as she concentrated. Her fingertips on his skin tingled and he forced his glance back to the fluorescent light and to the fly, now trapped and dying.

"So why a cop?" she asked, drawing back his attention. "What made you want to be sheriff?"

"Why a lawyer?"

She laughed and maneuvered the bobby pin in the lock. She glanced around the room and said, "Well, as you can see, it's quite glamorous." She thought a moment and then added, "No, I won't be flippant. It was my Uncle Arthur's doing." The first lock on Hick's handcuff clicked and she began turning the bobby pin clockwise. "Uncle Arthur came back to New York after the war to live with us. He had changed."

"War has a way of doing that to a man," Hick said, training his eyes on the string pull that hung down from the light.

"Well, it changed him. He was already an attorney when he left. He left for the war ready to put all the 'bad guys' in jail and came back from it more eager to keep the good ones out."

"What happened?"

"He was stationed at an internment camp in California. He watched those people lose everything without recourse. He figured someone needed to look out for the downtrodden. He went from prosecutor to Civil Rights activist. I admired him." She shrugged. "I wanted to be just like him."

"And then?"

"And then I worked hard, got into law school, passed the bar, and figured out that my lack of a male member would prevent me from ever really being anything other than clerk and coffee brewer." She glanced up at him. "Well, what about you? Were you that kid who always played cops and robbers?"

"No, I never wanted to be a cop. There are plenty of days I still don't want to be one."

"Then why are you?"

The second lock clicked and Hick quickly took his free hand and opened the handcuff and rubbed his wrist.

She remained close, peering into his face. "Well?"

Hick stepped back and lit another cigarette from the tip of the one he'd just finished. He offered Carol the pack, but she shook her head and remained standing before him with a questioning glance. He sighed. "It just kind of happened."

Carol frowned. "So, what did you want to be?"

"I guess I always figured I'd be a teacher, like my dad. But my grades kept me out of college and then the war ..."

"You were in the war?"

Hick dropped the first cigarette to the floor and stepped on it. "Yeah, I was in the war."

"So when you got home, you didn't want to teach anymore?"

Hick moved to the doorway, suddenly uncomfortable with all the questions. "When I got home, I realized I had nothing to teach." He put his hand on the doorframe and looked it over, then steadied himself and said, "It won't be easy to get out of here."

She crossed the room toward him. "He's not really going to let us go when this is all over with, is he?"

Hick stopped inspecting the door frame and closed his eyes. He saw Maggie's face and the faces of his sons. He sighed. "No. He's just trying to figure out a way he can get rid of us without anyone knowing about it. We can't count on him for any favors."

Carol shook her head slowly. "There are only so many planes flying into Memphis. Help won't be able to get here for hours." Realization crept into her eyes. "They won't reach us in time."

Turning to her, Hick saw she was pale but composed. There was no point in pretending so he told her, "If we're not out of this room pretty soon we're gonna have a problem."

20
Tuesday, July 20, 1954

Hick tossed the crumpled cigarette pack to the floor and rubbed his forehead in frustration. "Damn," he muttered after fiddling with the lock, the door knob, and the hinges. "There's got to be a way," he said, more to himself than to Carol.

She stood across the room, leaning against the wall, and watched him. "What time is it?" she asked.

"Close to 12:30."

"I wonder what time he'll be back."

"It all depends on how far away the caller was when they saw Enos. He couldn't already be back in Broken Creek. He hadn't been gone long enough when the call came in."

He turned back to the door and examined the hinges.

"Are you scared?" Carol asked.

Hick stopped and looked at her. He couldn't tell if she was frightened. She seemed calm in spite of the circumstances.

"I'm not afraid," he said. "And I'm getting home to my family come hell or high water."

He turned back to the door and reached toward it when it jerked open. The sudden motion caused Hick to jump back and Carol gasp. Royal stood in the doorway, his face flushed and excited. "You two gotta get, now!"

"Royal, we can't just walk out an unlocked door. Brewster will know you—"

"No!" Royal interrupted, urgency in his voice. "Brewster stopped at the drug store to get a Coke on his way out of town. I was in the back and he never saw me, but I heard him talking to some men. Said you was both outsiders stirring up the pot and that it was past time you were taught a lesson. Made sure they knew he was going to fetch Thad and wasn't gonna hurry home. He told them you was lock in here and that he wasn't planning on being back until after dark."

"That son of a bitch," Hick muttered shaking his head. "You really think they'll do anything?"

Royal rubbed the back of his neck. "I think they might. Most of the folks here in town are good people, but the ones he was talking to are pretty bad."

"How bad?" Hick asked.

"Well, one of them was my second cousin, Hoyt Smith. He's been in trouble with the law before." Royal hesitated. "I think he's been in trouble in Cherokee Crossing if I'm not mistaken."

Hick's face darkened. "I'm well acquainted with Hoyt."

"What do you think they would do?" Carol asked.

""After all the shootin' and burnin' last night," Royal said, "I don't know what to think. But Brewster gave them boys a green light to cause trouble, and nothing good can come from that. I got you both into this mess, and I'm getting' you out."

Carol stepped toward the door. "Where do we go?"

"You need to get back to Cherokee Crossing."

"No," Hick said. "There's help coming and they'll be looking for us here at the motel in Broken Creek. They're already on their way so it's too late to leave. We can't go. Not yet." He thought for a minute. "Can you get us to the motel or the Catholic Church without anyone seeing?"

Royal shook his head. "If they figure out you're gone, those will be the first places they'd think of."

"Any ideas, then?" Hick asked.

Royal thought for a moment and then nodded. "We need to bust this place up to make it look like you got out on your own. And then, someone owes me a favor and it'll be the last place Uncle Brewster'd think to look."

∾

White lace curtains fluttered in the breeze and a large grandfather clock chimed the half hour as Hick and Carol followed Royal into the manicured entry way of the large white house. Patsy, the young girl from the juke joint, wrung her hands.

"Why do I have to get involved, Royal?" Patsy followed him as he barged inside without hesitation.

He stopped and looked down at her. "Because you owe me, and I don't know where else to take 'em. I know your daddy and mama went to see your grandma in Marmaduke.

This is a matter of life and death. These people need your help."

She regarded Hick and Carol a moment. "Everyone was talking about these two in school. They say a lawyer from up north is messing things up and interfering with the sheriff. Aren't they the ones causing all the trouble?"

Royal's face grew red. "You want to know who's causing all the trouble? People like my Uncle Earl."

"Your Uncle Earl?" Patsy repeated, her brows drawn together in confusion. "But he's our sheriff."

"That don't mean he abides by the law any more than the next man," Royal said. He narrowed his eyes and looked at Patsy. "Hell, even a preacher will lie if the truth gets too much to handle."

Patsy's eyes grew wide. "What are you saying? Are you talking about my daddy?"

"I seen him, Patsy. I seen him yesterday at the station with Uncle Earl. They sat there, all those preachers, and right in the middle of 'em sat your daddy, listening to Uncle Earl saying he was gonna re-arrest Thad, and not a one of 'em stood up and said it was wrong. And they all know he's innocent. They're plotting about something. They're up to no good."

Patsy crossed her arms and hugged them to her chest. "I don't believe you."

"I don't care what you believe. I can't mistrust what I seen with my own eyes and heard with my own ears."

"But why would they do that to a little boy?"

"That's what we're trying to figure out," Hick spoke up.

"They're protecting someone. It could be anyone." He paused and asked Royal, "Those men in the room ... besides all being preachers was there anything they had in common? Are they related to Brewster?"

"No."

"So why would they go along with Brewster's plan? What would they gain from locking Thad up? It makes no sense," Carol said.

Royal shook his head. "I can't figure it out. It was just about every preacher in town ... except for that Catholic fella and a few others."

"And you didn't hear anything else?" Hick asked.

"The only thing I heard was Uncle Earl telling them the plans hadn't changed and that no highfalutin lawyer was gonna stop him. Then he started talking about getting rid of her and heading out to Miss Burton's house to re-arrest Thad and that's when I figured it'd be best to hide him and Miss Quinn away at the juke joint. I didn't waste any time when I heard what was in Uncle Earl's mind. I wisht now I'd stayed a little longer."

"But why the preachers?" Carol wondered. "What can they do?"

"They can turn public opinion against Thad," Hick said. "Down here a preacher is a powerful man. The public gets convinced Thad did it, and then the real culprit will be able to go about his business unmolested." He turned to Patsy. "When are your parents supposed to be home? I assume your daddy plans on preaching this Sunday."

"They'll be back Thursday or Friday."

"Why'd they go? Your grandma sick?"

"No, she's fine. Daddy said he just needed to get away."

"Away from what?" Royal asked.

"I don't know." Tears sprung up in Patsy's eyes. "You're right. Something's going on," she finally admitted. "Everyone's been unhappy. Daddy's been so upset that he even yelled at me. Then he told Mama they needed to get out of town. He wanted me to go, but I didn't want to miss school."

"How old are you?" Hick asked.

"Seventeen," Patsy mumbled.

"You're young, but you're old enough to know right from wrong. Are you sure you don't know something, anything, that might help us?"

Patsy reached up to a class ring on a chain around her neck and absentmindedly put it to her mouth. Sighing, she let the ring drop. "Everything was normal until last Wednesday."

"What happened Wednesday?" Royal asked.

She glanced at him. "It was all so strange. I woke up and Sheriff Brewster was in the kitchen talking to Daddy. It wasn't even light yet. He told Daddy, 'you have a stake in this, too' and Daddy was angry. He said he wouldn't have blood on his hands, and Brewster told him it was a little late for moralizing." Here she looked down at the floor and a fat tear rolled down her cheek. "They started to move so I ran back to my room." She shrugged. "I don't know what they were talking about, honest. I don't know anything. I just know that ever since, Daddy's been pacing the floors and not sleeping."

"What could be bothering him so much he'd leave town?" Hick wondered.

"We've got less than twenty-four hours to figure it out," Royal said.

"Shit," Hick muttered. He scratched the back of his neck and paced around the room. "A stolen truck, a jar of moonshine, and a whole town intent on covering for someone." He shook his head. "I don't get it."

"We need to look at the facts, piece by piece," Carol said. "We have a body and we have a weapon, in this case a truck. We know the crime was committed late Tuesday night or early Wednesday morning and we assume it was an accident. Is this correct?"

"To my way of thinking, yes," Hick replied. "The location of the accident and the moonshine in the truck leads me to think the driver was on his way home from the juke joint and he'd been drinking."

"So the question becomes, who would be driving the truck. Either Sutton was driving it himself or someone stole it. If the truck was stolen, then why?"

"Because they didn't have a car of their own?" Royal asked.

"That could be one reason," Carol said.

Hick turned to Patsy. "These kids at school … the ones you say go all the time—they all have cars?"

"Yes," Patsy said. "And they wouldn't go out there alone, I'm sure of it."

"We don't know they were alone," Hick said. "You know if any of your friends were out there Tuesday night?"

"No one said if they were. We had a big geometry test on Wednesday so I reckon most stayed home and studied."

"You notice any of your friends acting nervous or strange? Any have bruising on their face? Any limping around or looking like they've been in a fight ... or an accident?"

Patsy shook her head. "No. Everyone is fine."

"No one's been sick or missed school since Wednesday?" Hick asked.

"No," Patsy insisted, her voice rising. "There's nothing wrong with any of the kids at school, and if it happened late at night it couldn't be them because they all have curfews. I don't understand ... they got the one that did it. What are you trying to prove?"

Hick turned to Royal. "Maybe you ought to go out and have a word with Grover Sutton. Just tell him you need to clarify some of his testimony before tomorrow's hearing. See if you can trip him up or catch him in a lie."

"What are you getting at?" Patsy cried with a stomp of her foot. "I'll call Daddy and tell him what ya'll are trying to do."

"Tell him what?" Royal asked. "That we're trying to get at the truth. Is that such a bad thing?" He put on his hat and started out the back door. "I'll talk to Grover."

"I don't understand you," Patsy cried. "Why do you care?"

Royal spun around. "I have watched the town I thought I knew and the people I thought I trusted turn into a lying, vicious mob. Thad Burton is twelve years old. Twelve! Do you know what that prison camp will do to him? Do you have any idea what it will be like?"

"But what if it was one of my friends?" Patsy cried. "They'll go there, won't they? It won't be any better for them, will it?"

"No," Royal admitted. "But these 'friends' of yours … they don't think there's anything wrong with letting some poor kid take the rap for something he didn't do. They think it's fun to go driving their cars around the colored side of town and hollering out the windows and calling people names. They go to juke joints, they get in fights. They ain't the kind of folks you should be running around with."

The doorbell rang and everyone jumped at the sound. "I've got to get back to school," Patsy said, glancing nervously at the door. "My lunch hour is over."

Hick glanced out the front window and noticed a young man in a letterman's jacket on the porch.

"That Billy?" Royal asked.

Patsy nodded. The doorbell rang again and she added, "I've got to go, Royal. Am I just supposed to let these people stay here?"

"Yes, and don't tell anybody they're in here … especially Billy."

"But—"

"These people are here to help Thad. They ain't done nothing wrong. They are here to help find the truth, not cover up for someone else's crime. It's the ones that are trying to cover for someone—those are the ones we need to find and if you know something you ought to tell us."

Patsy stuck out her lip like a child. "Even if I did know something, I couldn't help you hurt one of my friends."

"Then you and your friends are helping to put an innocent boy away for six years," Royal said. He stuck his finger in her face and said, "You hide these two. We still have a deal. You don't say a word to nobody." His eyes flashed anger and he turned and started to open the back door.

"What's wrong with you, Royal?" Patsy cried. "Why is this so important?" The doorbell rang again and her eyes flitted to the front of the house.

Royal paused with his hand on the knob. "When you keep your mouth shut, and just shake your head behind closed doors and say, 'what a shame' you're as bad as those kids shootin' up houses." He shook his head. "I used to love you, Patsy. I reckon I never knew just what you were." He nodded at Hick. "I'll be back."

He walked out and left Hick and Carol with Patsy. She looked at them, took a deep breath, and closed her eyes. "I won't say anything to anyone about ya'll being here. A deal's a deal." With that, she turned, opened the front door, and slipped out. Hick and Carol watched her walk down the street with Billy.

21
Tuesday, July 20, 1954

Hick slammed another kitchen drawer in frustration. "Figures we'd be holed up at a preacher's house," he said to Carol. "Not a cigarette in sight."

She smiled, pulled a chair out, and sat at the kitchen table. "I could sure use one right now." She paused, and then asked, "That deputy ... you think he'll be okay? He was pretty upset."

Hick shrugged. "Hard to say. It's rough when you get disillusioned with people you care about."

"Are you speaking from experience?"

Hick turned to face Carol. "Yeah. I'm speaking from experience."

"When will Royal be back?" a voice from the doorway asked. They both whirled around to see Patsy wearing a worried frown.

"I have no idea," Hick said. "I thought you were at school."

She shook her head. "My head's bustin' open so I left." Opening a cabinet door, she peered inside. After a moment, her shoulders sagged. "We're out of aspirin."

"Why don't you sit down?" Carol suggested.

Patsy looked at them both and then sat across the table from Carol.

"You're worried about him?" Carol prodded.

Patsy looked down at her hands. "Royal's never spoke to me like that," she said in a teary voice. "I didn't do anything wrong."

"Well what did you think he'd—" Hick began, accusingly.

"Tell us about Royal," Carol interrupted, shooting Hick an angry glance.

Patsy put her head in her hands. "What about him?"

"Does Royal miss you?" Carol asked. "Does he dislike you running around with your friends because he wants to be with you?"

"No," Patsy said, shaking her head. "Royal and me are ancient history. He's the one that broke it off, not me."

"Is he right about your friends?" Hick asked. "He seems to think they're not the kind of people you should spend time with."

Patsy sighed. "Some of them can be a little wild," she admitted.

"What about Billy?" Hick asked.

"Billy?" Patsy repeated, looking up. She shook her head. "Billy likes to pretend he's tough. It's hard being the son of the President of the School Board."

"I can understand that," Hick said. "My daddy was the school principal."

Patsy offered him a small smile. "Then you know how it is. How hard it is when the kids call you 'teachers' pet' and all."

"I know it's hard, but it's no excuse for doing things you know ain't right. Like drinking moonshine and betting on roosters."

"But there's a whole bunch that do it," Patsy argued. "That's what I keep trying to tell Royal. Billy ain't any worse than the rest of the bunch."

"But he doesn't sound any better either," Carol said softly.

Patsy looked Carol in the eye. "He is better." She sighed. "He's just trying to fit in."

Hick sat down beside Patsy. "I want you to think real hard about this, Patsy. Are you sure there's no way any of the kids at school could have been driving Grover Sutton's truck the night that man was run down? He was killed on the same road as the juke joint that your friends all like to go to. Are you sure one of your friends didn't have a little too much to drink and then accidentally run that man over?"

"I don't know!" Patsy said in a tight voice. "I really don't. I don't think so because it doesn't make sense. All the boys work on their own cars. Why take someone's old truck when you have a perfectly good car? I'm just saying what I think. I don't know what ya'll want from me."

"But the kids at school knew about Sutton's truck? That the keys were left inside?" Hick persisted.

"Well, yes," Patsy answered. "Everyone knew. It wasn't a secret."

The door to the house opened and Royal burst in. His nose was bloodied and his face was smudged with dirt. He stalked across the room and threw his badge on the table. "I'm done," he said, his voice sad and resigned. He placed his gun beside the badge and then stood, looking at them as if he might cry.

Hick rose. "What happened?"

Royal shrugged. "I went out to see Sutton again like you said. I had a feeling there was more to the story than he was letting on."

"And?"

"And it took some 'persuading' but he spilled it."

Hick closed his eyes. "Oh, Royal. That's not the way—"

"Spare me." Royal held up his hands and looked at Hick with a dark frown. "I'm through with doing things the right way and expecting folks to be decent."

Hick noticed Royal was pointedly avoiding looking at Patsy. "What'd Sutton say?"

"Just what we expected. That Brewster ordered him to point the blame at Thad. Not necessarily say he done it for sure, just say enough to make it look reasonable for Brewster to bring him in."

"Why would Sutton do that for Brewster?" asked Carol.

"Because, contrary to what Willie Taylor says, ol' Deacon Sutton is a regular visitor to his still. Brewster promised Sutton that everyone in Broken Creek would know about it unless he did him this little favor."

Hick ran his hand through his hair in frustration. "So the moonshine jar in the truck was Sutton's after all?"

"I don't think so," Royal said. "Deacon Sutton says he never drinks outside the house. He's afraid he might be seen."

"You believe him?" Hick asked.

Royal rubbed his knuckles. "Yeah. I don't think he was in much of a mood to lie."

"Do you think he will testify to this in court?" Carol asked in an eager voice. "Will he admit under oath that Brewster coerced his testimony?"

Royal smiled a little to himself. "Yes, ma'am. I reckon he will."

"That will be the second nail in the fat bastard's coffin as far as the case against Thad is concerned," Carol said. "Coerced testimony and fabricated evidence. Things aren't looking too good for Brewster getting a conviction right now."

"I don't think kidnapping us and locking us in a store-room will help him much either," Hick added, with a wry smile.

Carol tapped her foot and said, "I need to get to my motel. I need to get that arrest warrant and witness statement."

"Hoyt Smith and a few other men are loitering around the jailhouse and you're supposed to be locked inside. I think you should stay out of sight, at least until sundown," Royal said.

"Sundown," Carol repeated. "What time is that?"

"This time of year about 8:30," Hick said.

Carol shook her head. "I can't wait that long. If the agents caught the 3:30 flight at the National Airport they'll be in Memphis around 5:30 and here in Broken Creek by 7:30 or 8:00. If I'm not at the motel, they won't know where to find me."

"I'm not sure I can persuade Hoyt and his friends to go on home. They've known me since I was a little boy. I can ask them to disperse, but they won't. They'll just laugh if I tell them they're loitering," Royal said. "I can get your brief-case for you, but I reckon you'll need to stay here. Uncle Earl was easy to get out of town, but there ain't much I can do to get them other fellas to move along."

"You got rid of Brewster? What do you mean?" Hick asked.

"Called in the tip to get him to go off after Thad," Royal said with a shrug.

As Hick listened to Royal, a sudden thought occurred to him. "Royal, did you call Miss Quinn's law firm in New York?"

Royal seemed surprised. He looked at Carol. "Well, yeah. I thought everyone knew that."

Hick sank into a chair. "No. No, we did not know that. What put it in your mind?"

"Butch Simmons, the reporter, came to the station right after you left that first night wanting to know who you was and what you was doing. When I mentioned all those points you brought up he just whistled and said it looked like Thad was getting the shaft. I asked him what I should do and he said there wasn't a damned thing I could do to help a colored boy down here."

"I didn't like that one bit, but I knew he was right about one thing: any lawyer the local court might appoint wouldn't be much help." Royal shifted a little and frowned. "Next day, I was at the barber shop and picked up a *LOOK* magazine.

I saw a story in it about some colored girls in Arizona going to the white school and figured a northern lawyer would likely be more help than a court appointed one down here. They named a law firm in the article so I drove out to Pocahontas and made a call from the sheriff's office." He grinned. "I'm sure there'll be hell to pay when they see the phone bill. Honestly, I didn't reckon anyone would answer on a Friday night, but Miss Quinn was still working. She told me she'd see what she could do."

Carol and Hick and Patsy all stared at Royal. "I thought you said you weren't bright," Hick said with a laugh.

Royal look confused and then a smile covered his face. "Hmmm. I reckon I'm smarter than I thought."

"I reckon you are," Hick agreed. "Listen, if we're going to have to lay low for a while I need you to do a few things."

"What?"

"First, I need you to get word to my wife that I'm okay, and I'll be here longer than I thought. Maybe a day or two. Call Adam at the Cherokee station and have him tell her."

"I'll go to the phone booth at the drug store. It's pretty private."

"Good," Hick said. "Also, tell the Father Grant what's going on and to keep an eye out for Enos and Thad. Ask him to let us know if he hears any news."

Royal nodded and Hick continued, "Also, hang around the motel and look for any strangers … anyone from out of town. There's some politicians and agitators coming in and I'd like to know how many and what kind of trouble they intend to make. And be watching for some men from the FBI or the Department of Justice. When they show up, bring them here."

Royal started to hurry out the door when Carol called, "And kid, don't forget my brief case. It should be on the bed if Brewster left it behind."

"Wait." Hick handed Royal his badge. "Put this back on. At least for now. If you see someone, just tell 'em you need to know what their business is in town. Ain't no reason they shouldn't be forthcoming with the law about it."

Royal picked up the badge, and looked at it in his hand. His eyes flicked up to Patsy and back down. He fastened the badge on his shirt. "Anything else?"

"Yeah," Hick replied. "Take this." He handed Royal his gun. "It'll look strange if you don't have your weapon."

Royal sighed and holstered his pistol.

"One more thing," Carol said, casting a quick glance at Hick, "we need a pack of cigarettes."

22

Tuesday, July 20, 1954

Hick paced back and forth across the room. He wasn't used to sitting back and waiting for someone else to do the leg work and, without a cigarette to keep his hands busy, his nerves were getting the better of him.

"Sit down," Carol complained. "You're making me jumpy."

He walked to the window. "What the hell do you think is going on?"

"You gave the kid a pretty formidable list. I'm sure he's just following instructions."

Hick ran his hand through his hair. "Dammit! I don't like this waiting around."

Carol rose and put her hand on his shoulder. "There's nothing you can do. You might as well sit down and try to relax before you drive us all crazy."

He sat across from her. "Now what?"

"Now, we wait," she said with a smile.

"Where'd the girl, Patsy, say she was going?" Hick asked, shifting in his chair and looking out the window.

"She went to the drug store for aspirin," Carol replied.

Hick glanced at the clock. It was close to four o'clock. "She should be home soon shouldn't she?"

Voices were heard in front of the house and Hick moved to the window. Patsy was in front of the house beside the gate with Billy Davis. He kissed her cheek and walked away and Patsy walked up sidewalk toward the porch.

Carol's brow knit. "Hillbilly, you don't think she'd..."

Hick shrugged. "I have no idea. But it's not like we could imprison her in her own home. Royal trusts her so we'll just have to trust his judgment."

"Do you?"

Hick sat back down. "I do. I thought he was nothing but a dumb country bumpkin when I first met him, but he's got the potential to be a really top-notch law enforcement officer. I don't think I gave him enough credit."

"No one ever does," a voice said and Hick and Carol turned to see Patsy enter the room.

"Here," she said, handing Hick a pack of Lucky Strikes. "Royal saw me at the drug store and sent these. He got a hold of your deputy and he said everything is fine at home. Also Royal told me to tell you he'll be at the motel for the time being." She walked to the sink and filled a glass of water and then took two aspirin. She put the glass in the sink and turned to face Hick and Carol. "He was telling the truth," she said in a voice of sad wonder.

"What are you talking about?" Carol asked.

"His story," she said. "What he told us ... I didn't believe a word of it so I walked past the police station. There were five men just standing around, five men my daddy tells me to stay far away from. They whistled when I walked past and called me 'sweetheart' and 'baby.' I told them they'd better be careful or they'd end up in that jail they were standing in front of."

She shuddered, then continued, "Mr. Hoyt Smith walked right up to me and winked. He told me plainly that he intended to be inside that jail just as soon as the sun went down."

Hick took a deep breath to control the anger welling up inside. He flipped open the Zippo lighter roughly, lit two cigarettes, and handed one to Carol.

"Then what?" he asked letting the cigarette smoke slowly seep from his nostrils.

"I said the jail's closed up at night and he laughed and said business hours didn't apply to him." She crossed her arms. "I hate that man, the way he looks at me and the other girls." She shuddered again.

"Then what happened?" Carol asked.

"I got away from there as fast as I could and got inside the drug store for my aspirin. Thank God Billy skipped baseball practice. I didn't want to walk back past those men alone." Patsy bit her lip. "I like ya'll, I really do. So, I'm going to tell you something." She paused. "I didn't say nothing to Billy about you, but while I was at the drug store I called my daddy."

"You what?" Hick said.

"I called him. I told him what Royal told me about that little colored boy."

"What did he say?"

"Nothing," she said. She covered her face with her hands. "He didn't say a thing."

"Did you tell him about us being here?" Carol asked.

"No," Patsy replied. "I just asked him if what Royal said was true. About him being there that night, at the police station with the sheriff, and those other preachers. I asked him if it was true they were working with the sheriff to get that little colored boy in trouble for something he didn't do. And the line was silent. He didn't answer me."

"So what did you say?" Carol asked.

Patsy began to cry. "I told him I was ashamed to be his daughter and hung up." She looked from Hick to Carol. "You want to know why me and Royal aren't together anymore? It's because my daddy was always on Royal, always after him to better himself, to be something. He always said Royal wasn't half good enough for me and then Royal started believing him." She sighed. "My daddy wants me to be with a man who has a future. I know Billy Davis is going to be a great success someday and he treats me right. But Billy's never really had to work for anything he has." She closed her eyes. "Next to Royal, Billy's like a spoiled little boy."

Patsy's face grew puzzled. "I always thought my daddy knew best. I've always trusted and believed him." She shook her head. "And then Daddy turns around and does this to an innocent little colored kid." Patsy walked to the window and looked outside. She absentmindedly tugged at the ring on the chain around her neck and bit her lip. "I've never known Royal to strike another person. And now he hit Mr. Sutton." She shook her head. "No one is acting right." She closed her eyes and a tear slid down her cheek. "I've got a terrible headache. If ya'll don't mind, I'm going to lie down."

She left the room and Hick began to pace again, unable to sit still.

"Okay, Hillbilly," Carol said, "We need to figure this out. Why the elaborate frame job and why is everyone going along? You think Brewster's got something on all of them?"

"I don't know," Hick said, shaking his head. "Rational, civilized men suddenly stooping to this sort of unethical behavior." He ran a hand through his hair. "I just don't get it."

Carol rubbed her temples. "Well, I'm starting to get a headache myself. You hungry?"

"Starving," Hick said.

Peeking in the icebox, Carol said, "I could scramble some eggs."

"That sounds perfect," Hick answered. He opened a couple of cabinets, found a skillet, and set it on the stovetop.

He watched as she tied on an apron and cracked some eggs into a skillet. After a few moments, he said, "So, if you don't mind my asking … why aren't you married?"

She smiled and flounced the apron. "I look perfectly domestic at this moment, don't I?" She turned back to the eggs and gave them a stir. "Once you marry you're expected to settle down and raise a family. I have nothing against women who do that. I'm just not ready to give up what I set out to do. I've fought too long and too hard to be recognized as a bona fide attorney."

"You have something to prove," Hick said.

"Yes," she paused for a moment. "Yes, I do."

"And you've not met anyone who understands that, who can respect that?"

She regarded him a moment, a hint of surprise in her eyes, then turned back to the skillet. "I thought, at one point I might have," she finally answered. "But, no."

"His loss," Hick mumbled.

A smile lit up her face as she put the eggs on plates and sat them on the table. "Maybe it's his loss," she said in a false, light voice. "Or maybe his salvation. You haven't tasted my cooking."

Hick ate a bite and then asked, "Interesting that Billy Davis is Ike's son. I'm not sure I made that connection."

"Yes, it is interesting," Carol agreed. "But Billy was in school the next day, uninjured, and has a car. I don't think we have enough to move him onto any kind of list of suspects."

"You're right," Hick agreed. "And that list is pretty small, although I'm surprised that Hoyt Smith is back in town. Last I heard he'd gone off to Oklahoma."

Carol leaned back in her chair. "Tell me about this Hoyt Smith. He sounds like a real son of a bitch."

Hick sat his fork down. "The first year I was sheriff, he and his brother broke into the Cherokee Crossing post office. I brought them in and it went before a federal grand jury. The charge didn't stick."

Carol motioned with her fork for Hick to continue.

"I knew Mule and Hoyt Smith were in town and noticed a broken window at the post office. I went inside and saw that someone had busted into the mail boxes. I assumed it was the Smith boys because they were known trouble makers here in Broken Creek, and I reckon I wanted to show them they couldn't get away with the same in Cherokee. I found them headed back home and pulled them over. Unfortunately, I arrested them outside my jurisdiction. Since I never saw them at the post office, I was technically not in 'fresh pursuit.' Adam was working on getting the right paperwork, but I got in a hurry. I knew they'd get rid of the evidence. Sheriff Earl Brewster made a great show of how sorry he was that I'd acted in such a rash manner, saying he'd have taken care of them when they got back to town. Nobody believed that, but he was convincing enough that all charges were dropped."

"And you say they're related to Brewster?"

"Cousins."

She rolled her eyes. "Clearly, Brewster has a history of covering for his family."

"It seems to be a bad habit with him," Hick agreed. "And I hope it's a habit we'll be able to help him break." He drummed his fingers on the table. "We know what Brewster has on Sutton, but what about the rest?"

"I can't believe the whole town drinks moonshine. What else could it be?"

"You'd be surprised the kind of trouble you can get yourself into in a small town. Marital infidelities, being where you shouldn't be, getting magazines you ought not read. It doesn't have to be something illegal. Public humiliation can be every bit as bad as jail time."

"I guess there really are no secrets in a small town," Carol said.

Hick sighed and got a faraway look in his eyes. He rose, walked over, and opened the back door to get some air. "There are plenty of secrets in small towns," he said, turning back to Carol. "They're just harder to keep."

The sound of the front door opening drew their attention, and they both looked to the front of the house. "You think Royal's back already?" Carol said.

"Patsy?" a voice called out.

Seconds later the door to the kitchen swung open and a man entered the room. He stopped short and stared. "Who are you?"

The man was older, somewhere in his sixties. He was disheveled and frantic, as if he'd dropped everything and rushed over.

Hick's back was ramrod straight, senses on full alert. "I could ask you the same thing," he said.

The man puffed up. "I am the Reverend Michael Russell. This is my home. Now, again, I ask, who are you and what have you done with my daughter?"

"I'm Sheriff Hick Blackburn, and I'm from Cherokee Crossing. This is attorney Carol Quinn, from New York City."

Reverend Russell looked from Hick to Carol and back again, brows knit in confusion. "But why are you here ... in my kitchen?"

"They're here to and try and help that little boy you and all your friends want to put in jail," Patsy said with a sniff. Her eyes were swollen and her nose red as she pushed past her father and into the kitchen.

Her father started toward her. "Patsy, you don't understand."

She swallowed a sob, stiffened, and backed away from him. "I understand plenty, Daddy! I might not understand why, but I know you lied and you lied to hurt someone. He's just a child." She wiped her nose on her sleeve. "Ya'll are nothing but a bunch of liars and bullies."

Reverend Michael Russell exhaled and closed his eyes. His shoulders slumped and he pulled out a chair and sat heavily at the table opposite Carol. He ran a hand over his face and looked up at his daughter. "You're right. What we conspired to do—it was unconscionable. Every man in that room knew Thad was innocent. But, we each had a 'role' to play."

"What do you mean by role?" Hick narrowed his eyes. "What the hell is going on here?"

He clasped his hands on the table and stared at them. Finally, he took a deep breath and said, "I guess my part in the sordid charade is over, and I'm glad of it." He turned to Hick. "Broken Creek's been under the thumb of Earl Brewster for over a dozen years. He has a way of doing 'favors' for those he thinks may be useful to him in the future, and when the time comes he isn't shy about demanding repayment."

Carol leaned forward. "We suspected it was something like that. But what do you mean by repayment?"

"Little favors here and there. In this particular case, it means telling my congregation that people like Thad are different. I was instructed to plant the notion that colored people aren't like them—that they don't value life, that they have no conscience. Lies like that are pretty easy for some white folks to swallow."

Hick frowned. "And if you make it convincing enough, they'll believe anything. Even a cockamamie story about a little colored boy stealing a truck he can't drive, running someone over, and then going to school the next day as if nothing ever happened." His brow knit and he rubbed his temple as if he was the one with the headache. "The question is, who the hell is Brewster covering for? And why criminalize a whole community?"

"Covering for someone?" Reverend Russell repeated. "I suppose he is covering for someone ... but that's not why he's doing this."

"What do you mean?" Carol asked.

Reverend Russell shifted uncomfortably and licked his lips. "Earl Brewster is intent on holding Thad Burton up as an example of why colored folks can't be trusted. Why they can't be trusted in the community..." He looked at Hick and Carol pointedly. "And most certainly why they can't be trusted with the white kids in school."

"In school?" Carol repeated. "So this is about integrating the Broken Creek schools after all. I don't understand. Why the sudden need to make an issue of something the town had already accepted?"

"Because an opportunity presented itself," Russell said.

"An opportunity for what?" Hick asked.

"Think about it. It's an election cycle and desegregation is on the mouths and lips of every man in the south. Senator John Wesley Richardson hails from this very town and the democratic primary is close. Too close. He's made desegregation the cornerstone of his campaign to try and help people forget some of his past progressive ideas, and he's whipped all of Arkansas, from Little Rock to Texarkana into a frenzy over this issue. And then suddenly his home-town decides to desegregate?"

Carol's eyes sparked and she glanced at Hick. "And suddenly Thad Burton becomes the face of all their baseless prejudices. He becomes the tangible evil they've been taught to fear all their lives."

"Exactly," Reverend Russell said. "They can use him tomorrow night at their rally to illustrate why desegregation will destroy society. And then when Ike Davis publicly withdraws his support—"

"What about this Davis?" Hick interrupted. "What's Brewster got on him?"

"On Ike Davis?" Russell asked. "I can't imagine he has any secrets for Brewster to exploit. He is not the sort of man who needs favors from Sheriff Brewster. Ike is worried about the welfare of the student body in light of what he has been led to believe about Thad." He shook his head. "It has all worked out very conveniently for the senator. All the papers will be here and the story of Broken Creek's decision to halt desegregation will be big news—and good news for Senator Richardson's campaign."

Carol shook her head. "So Thad Burton is suddenly very important."

"I wonder what's in it for Brewster?" Hick said. "There has to be something."

The Reverend Russell shrugged. "I can't say for sure. If you're Sheriff Brewster and you have a high profile gubernatorial candidate coming to your little town one week before a statewide primary, you finally have your chance to catch his eye, to get noticed."

Hick frowned. "And if you can derail the desegregation of a school system by falsely arresting a helpless, colored boy, maybe the new governor would be inclinded to pay you back for your help."

"Exactly," said Russell. "Brewster's ambitious. If he can take a town that was on the brink of integrating their schools and turn it into a hot bed of racial unrest, he will have the senator's gratitude to say the least."

"Despicable," Carol said, her voice almost a growl.

"And all Broken Creek's preachers are fixin' to just go along with this?" Hick asked.

"We all had the same orders. Plant fear in the hearts of the townsfolk regarding colored people, because fear will always turn to hate. After the hate starts to grow, point out things like desegregation will cause inter-marriage and inter-marriage will create a mongrel race of half-breeds. Tell them their women are in danger and that a black man touching a white woman is an abomination."

"And the people in the pews, they'll believe this non-sense?" Carol asked.

"Some will and some won't. But then, the shopkeepers will say the colored kids are robbing them blind and the banker will say the colored folks aren't paying their bills. These things will add up. Start with Thaddeus Burton and amplify the innuendo. There is no standard of truth in the court of public opinion."

"Daddy! How could you?" Patsy pulled a dishcloth off a peg by the sink and wiped her nose.

Carol looked at the reverend in disgust. "And not one of you was man enough to defend that poor kid."

Michael Russell seemed tired. "Brewster reminded us that it was in all our best interests for Thad to plead guilty on Wednesday, not just his."

Hick shook his head. "Tell me, Russell, what kind of miracle cover-up did Brewster perform for you?"

"Not me," Reverend Russell said. "My son, Bob, God rest his soul."

Patsy gasped. "What are you talking about?"

Russell looked at his daughter, sadness was written across his face. "I had four children," he said. "Patsy here is the youngest, by far. My three older children are all boys and Bob was the second. My other two, they always seemed to do the right thing. They got good grades, went to church. They never gave us a minute of trouble. But Bob was different."

"I assume Bob was not a model citizen?" Carol asked.

Russell shook his head. "Bob was a good kid, but he was stupid and reckless. He got in with the wrong crowd. He and some friends broke into the General Store some years back and hurt the owner pretty bad."

Hick remembered his conversation with Willie Taylor at the moonshine still. "And you let Hap Taylor take the blame."

Russell's eyebrows shot up. He was speechless for a moment, but finally nodded. A defiant glimmer came into his eyes and his lips thinned into a bitter line. "It's not like Hap was an innocent lamb. He was bootlegging his daddy's moonshine and driving like a maniac through town. It was just a matter of time before he killed someone."

"So to your way of thinking, you were doing the public a favor by protecting your boy and letting Brewster arrest an innocent man?"

"In a word, yes. The town was better off with Hap behind bars and Bob had so much potential—so much to live for."

"Why Hap?" Hick asked. "Why didn't Brewster just bring in Willie?"

"Because Willie performs a service for the town and Brewster gets a cut of every jar of moonshine that degenerate sells. Arresting Hap was just Brewster's way of reminding Willie who's in charge."

"What do you mean Brewster gets a cut?" Hick asked.

"Earl Brewster won't go near Willie and for good reason. I think Willie would kill him on sight. But Brewster sends his deputies out to see Willie every month or so and Willie hands them some cash … just enough to keep the law from bothering his still or shutting down his operation."

"His deputies?" Hick asked, casting a glance at Patsy. "Royal Adkins one of these 'bill collectors?'"

"Royal for the last month or so. Before him Mitch Lackey, before him Bud Gibson. The practice has gone on for years, since Earl was a deputy and his brother was sheriff. The difference now is our previous Sheriff Brewster and Willie were on friendly terms. Donald Brewster is not quite the power monger his brother Earl seems to be."

"Son of a bitch," Hick grumbled. "That damned kid lied to me."

"Who? Royal Adkins?" Michael Russell asked. He looked at Hick with a sneer and said, "Royal Adkins wants to be the next sheriff of Broken Creek, Arkansas. There's nothing he'd like better than to take Brewster down."

Hick's mind reeled as he recalled Royal coming to him for help. Was there more to Royal's request than just wanting to help Thad? Troubled, he turned to Michael Russell to finish the story. "So what happened to your son? Where is Bob now?"

The Reverend's eyes hardened. "Justice was served. Bob died of pneumonia less than a month after Hap went to jail."

"Yeah, life's tough," Carol said with no sympathy. "And that doesn't excuse your current behavior one iota."

The reverend wearily closed his eyes. "I would describe my current behavior as 'inexcusable.'"

"So what about the others? What's Brewster got on them?"

Michael Russell stared at Hick in silence. Glancing at his daughter, he finally said, "I don't know what Brewster has on them. That is a subject we never discuss with one another."

"Is there anyone in this town that's honest?" Hick asked in aggravation.

"You'd have to look high and low," Russell admitted.

"Well, ya'll preachers are sure doing a fine job teaching the golden rule," Hick said with a dark frown. "So everyone is in on this scheme?"

"Not everyone," Russell said. "Not everyone has something to hide. But if you have a secret, Brewster's like a bloodhound. He'll find it and he'll use it against you." Russell shook his head. "Those of us who owe him, we sat in that room like mindless buffoons and each agreed to do our part."

Carol turned to Hick. "So what do we do now?"

"I don't know," Hick said with a shake of his head. "It's clear Brewster's got his boot on the neck of a lot of folks in this town. We can't beat them all into confessing."

The sound of the front door opening carried into the kitchen and Royal burst into the room. He stopped when he saw the Reverend Russell. "Reverend," he said in a cold voice.

"Hello, Royal," the reverend replied with equal coldness.

Royal turned to Hick. "Thad's in town. Brewster's got him in a holding cell at the courthouse. He locked up Enos for aiding and abetting."

"Aiding and abetting?" Hick exclaimed. "Enos was bringing him back."

Steps sounded behind him, and an older man in a suit appeared in the doorway behind Royal.

"Uncle Arthur!" Carol cried and ran into his arms.

Royal smiled. "Your friend is here."

Hick did not smile back. "Royal, you and I have some things to discuss."

23

Tuesday, July 20, 1954

As soon as Hick and Royal were in the small enclosed porch behind the house, Hick grabbed Royal by the collar and gave him a shaking. "I want you to tell me the truth about something," he said through gritted teeth.

Royal's eyes widened with shock. "What's wrong?"

"You ever collect extortion money from Willie Taylor?"

Royal's eyes narrowed in confusion. "What do you mean by extortion money?" Then his eyes widened and a slow look of realization settled on his features. "I reckon so," he admitted after a pause. "Uncle Earl sent me out there a time or two to collect Willie's 'monthly premium'. Said that's the way it's always been done."

"Dammit Royal, what were you thinking?" Hick said giving Royal a final shake before releasing him. "Your Uncle Earl's an elected official. That's a federal offense."

"It didn't even occur to me to question it." Royal sighed. "So much about Uncle Earl bothered me, it just seemed like one more thing I wasn't supposed to think about. One more thing he told me to just shut up and take care of. You gonna turn me in?"

"I don't know," Hick said. "And I don't know if I can trust you. You told me you wanted to be sheriff of this town. How do I know you're not using me and this whole situation to get Brewster's job."

"I don't want the job," Royal said, looking Hick in the eye. "When I said earlier I was done with it all, I meant it. When this is all over I'm leaving Broken Creek."

"Why should I believe you?"

"I've been up front about everything but Willie's money." Royal said. "You came to me, I didn't come to you. When we figured out what Brewster was up to, I made up my mind I wanted to get Thad some justice. That's the truth whether you believe me or not."

Carol Quinn entered the porch and leaned against the wall. "We may not have a choice, Hillbilly. We need this kid. And, don't forget, he saved our lives."

Hick turned a questioning glance on Royal and studied him. "I'm on the fence."

Royal shrugged. "I don't know what I can do."

"Sheriff," a voice said from the doorway. Patsy stood there wringing her hands. Her brow was knit and her mouth wore a small pout. "Royal Adkins is an honest man. What my daddy said to you … don't forget, he's never liked Royal on account of me." She paused. "I'd say Royal Adkins is honest to a fault."

"I don't see how that's possible," Hick returned, unconvinced.

"You don't know him," Patsy said, her voice trembling. "You don't know anything about him."

"Patsy," Royal interrupted, but she continued.

"You don't know what it was like for him growing up here in this town without a daddy. You don't know how hard people were on his mama. Nothing was given to Royal, ever. He worked hard for everything he ever had, and that wasn't much."

Hick raised his eyebrows and turned to Royal.

Shrugging, Royal said, "My daddy left us when I was two and my mama never found out what happened to him. She worried over him for weeks and finally figured he wasn't coming back so she went to work in the bakery. She begged Uncle Earl on her dying bed to take me as a deputy. He agreed, but after she died, he made it clear that he only promised to hire me. He never promised not to fire me." Royal sighed. "It's on account of I ain't bright. Uncle Earl likes to point out that only a dumb ass graduates high school when he's twenty-two. I didn't graduate until this past May. Mama died the next week."

Patsy shook her head. "The reason it took you three extra years to graduate is because you worked every day before and after school to help your mama pay the rent." She turned to Hick. "He'd come to school in the summers hot and sweaty and the kids would make fun of him. They hadn't done anything all morning but eat their Corn Flakes and get dressed. Royal'd come in and he'd already put in a good three hours work. He never got to play football or baseball like the other kids. He's worked since he was a little boy." Patsy held her head high and looked at her father who had joined them on the porch. "Some might call him poor white trash because of it." She shifted her gaze to Royal. "But I don't."

Michael Russell frowned. "Royal Adkins is from the wrong side of town. He's not the kind of boy for a girl like you."

"I don't believe you," she said looking at her father with a quizzical expression. "I doubt everything you ever told me because of what I've learned here today."

The Reverend Russell crossed his arms. "Young lady, you will speak to me with respect."

Patsy's eyes filled with tears. "When a boy has a father who can protect him, like Bob had, life is easy. Sometimes it's too easy. You let someone else's son go to jail for something Bob did. You're trying to help the sheriff put another little boy in jail for something he didn't do. And you ask me to speak to you with respect?" She shook her head. "I can't. No, sir. I have more respect for Royal Adkins than I'll ever have for you." She turned on her heel, pushed through the door and let the screen slam shut behind her.

Reverend Russell, his face worn and tired, sighed and walked back into to the kitchen. Hick watched him lower himself into a chair as if his bones were so tender they might break on contact.

"Sheriff, I want to help Thad for Thad's sake," Royal said, drawing Hick's attention back from the sorrowful man inside. "I grew up on the colored side of town and Thad's mama done our washing because my mama didn't have time on account of her job." His lips thinned into a bitter line.

"Colored folks are the only ones in Broken Creek with less than we had. And Ida Burton is a God-fearing woman and a good one. Help me help Thad and when this is all over you can turn me over to the Bureau or do whatever you see fit."

"That won't be necessary," Arthur Vance said, stepping out on the enclosed porch.

They all turned to him. "If you would be willing to testify against your sheriff, I can guarantee you immunity. Let me warn you, though, if you do you'll be hard pressed to find a welcome anywhere in this town."

"I'm ready to be shed of it. Never had much of a welcome in this hell hole anyway," Royal said.

Arthur Vance was soft spoken but intense. Removing his glasses and cleaning them with a handkerchief he looked at the faces around him.

"We need to discuss all of the particulars—what charges Sheriff Brewster has brought against Thaddeus Burton, and, most importantly, why."

Carol frowned and stubbed out a cigarette angrily. "I still don't have my paperwork," she fumed, glaring at Royal.

"Uncle Earl must have took your briefcase," Royal said. "It wasn't in your room."

"Well, if you'd given me a minute to get what I needed to have—" She began in an angry voice.

"No matter," Arthur Vance interrupted as he ushered the group back into the kitchen. "From what Deputy Adkins told me on the way, there is very little real evidence against Thaddeus Burton. The real question here is what Sheriff Earl Brewster is about—he is the reason I'm here and not one of my agents. It is clear we are dealing with egregious color of law violations." He sat at the table and indicated everyone should do the same. "But, this sheriff isn't what interests me. I would not have made the trip if we were only dealing with a crooked sheriff. I am very interested in the fact that State Senator John Wesley Richardson is involved."

"Why is that?" Hick asked.

"Senator Richardson is an opportunist. Becoming governor would give him just the kind of power he craves, the power to thwart, not only Brown vs. Board of Education, but the power to continue to suppress the colored vote. He's just the kind of man the Civil Rights section of the Justice Department needs to take down to become a full division of the Bureau." He looked at his niece who watched every move he made with open admiration. "And he's also just the kind of man the Civil Rights section was founded to fight against. The kind of man who craves power and runs roughshod over others without a second thought. The kind of man I joined the Justice Department to stop."

"Getting the boy and his father out of jail will not be a problem," he continued with a dismissive wave of his hand. "His arrest seems to be nothing more than Brewster's way of asserting his dominance over the colored population in town. From what I gathered looking into matters before I left Washington, the arrest of Thaddeus Burton is not an isolated incident. It seems that Earl Brewster has engaged in a pattern of harassment against numerous individuals, both white and colored. But I'm not after a two-bit sheriff in a ten cent town." He leaned back in his chair and looked at the people gathered around. "In fact, I believe that Brewster is nothing more than a tiny cog in large, corrupt machine. What I want to know is, did Senator John Wesley Richardson make this sheriff any offers or promises."

"What kind of offers?" Hick asked.

"There are many things a rich, powerful man could do for Brewster. He could offer him money, prestige, a better position. And in return Brewster can help him. It's crucial I learn if there has been discussion about suppressing the colored vote for the gubernatorial primary here in Broken Creek. That," he said with a tap of his finger on the table top, "is the matter in which I am most interested." Arthur studied Royal and Hick. "Perhaps, if you two could bring me the gentlemen Sheriff Brewster has engaged for this evening's mischief at the jailhouse …"

Hick nodded and glanced at Royal. "We can do that."

Arthur leaned back in his chair and regarded the two lawmen before him. "This could be dangerous."

"Just tell us what's in your mind," Hick said, holding Arthur's gaze. "I'd love nothing more than to see Brewster go down."

24
Tuesday, July 20, 1954

A shed behind the Broken Creek police station contained a canoe for water rescues, a tractor, a lawn mower, snow shovels, and other miscellaneous items that law enforcement in small towns are obliged to use on occasion. After insuring that Hoyt Smith and his two friends remained loitering on the sidewalk in front of the building, keeping busy with cigarettes and trying to drink enough courage to do Earl Brewster's bidding, Hick and Royal hid inside the shed and kept watch from a small window.

The sun still lit the horizon, but as the pink glow slowly diminished and the evening deepened, Hick and Royal became more alert. A breeze kicked up and late July lightning bugs rose from the ground near the tree line at the back of the lot. The sound of cicadas was replaced with that of crickets and, finally, when the stars became faint pinpricks in the sky, Hick noticed a shadow move toward the back of the station.

He nudged Royal and they watched the man pour liquid

on the ground around the building. He emptied a container and his companion handed him another.

"Only two shadows?" Royal whispered. "I wonder where the other fella is."

"Maybe he got cold feet," Hick said. "Keep an eye out."

Finally, after several containers were emptied, Hick watched as Hoyt stepped back and pulled something from his pocket. He threw it and a wall of flame whooshed bright orange, then quickly died down until only a line of fire surrounded the back of the station. The man with Hoyt tossed brush along the fire line and the air became filled with the choking smell of burning timber. Hoyt stood back and crossed his arms as his companion gave him a celebratory clap on the shoulder.

As the men stood, silhouetted against the growing flames, Hoyt's companion handed him a jar of moonshine and Hoyt took a long, slow drink. He tossed the jar against the jailhouse and it crashed against the door and shattered. The flames slowly licked at the back porch of the jailhouse, the dry wood succumbing to the flames. An opportune breeze and a rug lying before the door were the last ingredients needed for the porch to collapse. Hick noticed that smoke had begun to seep from beneath the roofline of the jail and realized that the fire had made its way into the evidence room. The amount of paperwork stored there insured that the jail would be quickly reduced to rubble.

Hick nodded and he and Royal crept out of the shed and made their way toward the flames, where the two men were distracted by fire, bravado, and a day's worth of drinking.

Royal pounced first and knocked Hoyt's companion to the ground where the two men scuffled, rolling closer toward and then away from the line of fire. Hoyt turned and his eyes widened at the sight of Hick. Hoyt charged and they slammed to the ground. Stunned by the hard earth on his back, Hick felt the air go out of him and, for a brief moment, couldn't think straight. Then Hoyt's fist crashed against his cheekbone sending stars whirling behind Hick's eyelids. Hick blinked, cleared his mind, and shoved hard against Hoyt, sending him reeling backwards. Hick scrambled to his feet and grabbed Hoyt by the front of his shirt. It was impossible to deny how good it felt when Hick's fist met the hard bone of Hoyt's jaw. Hoyt sprawled backward and Hick was on him. Grabbing his arm and twisting it up hard and fast behind his back, Hick hissed, "Go ahead and resist. Nothing would give me more pleasure than to beat the hell out of you."

Instead Hoyt slumped to the ground and Hick clapped the handcuffs Royal had given him around Hoyt's wrists. Blood dripped from a cut near Hick's eye and mingled with sweat from exertion and the heat of the flames. He wiped his face with his sleeve, stood, and looked over to see Royal straddling Hoyt's companion, who was now face down in the dirt. Royal pulled out his cuffs, slapped them closed around the man's wrists, and then hoisted himself off a narrow, rumpled backside.

"Get up." Royal commanded as he brushed dirt from his hands.

"You know him?" Hick asked.

"Know him?" Royal repeated, wiping dirt from his shirt. "Hell, I'm related to him. Ain't that right, Cousin Dan?"

Royal's cousin scrambled to his knees and looked up at the deputy with a dark, sullen expression.

Hick heaved Hoyt Smith to his feet in the bright orange glow of the burning building. Flames licked up the walls and a window shattered from the heat. Something caught inside and flames shot through the window with a roar. "Let's get these two over to Vance," Hick shouted. "We need to get out of here before any more of your kin show up."

"You can't take me nowhere," Hoyt protested in the defiant tone of one who knows how to manipulate the law. "You ain't got jurisdiction in this town."

"You want me to leave you in a cell and go find the sheriff?" Hick asked, putting his face close to Hoyt's. "I'll be glad to escort you inside where you can wait."

The clanging bells of the Volunteer Fire Department sounded in the distance as Hoyt's narrow gaze slid toward the jailhouse. The back of the building was now fully engulfed, and Hoyt swallowed hard.

"I didn't think so," Hick said. "Besides, Royal's got all the jurisdiction we need."

"Where're we going?" Hoyt asked with a scowl as Hick pushed him into the back seat of Arthur Vance's hired car. "What are you—" Hick slammed the door on Hoyt's questions as Royal deposited Cousin Dan next to Hoyt.

The two lawmen climbed in the front seat as the firetruck drew closer. Hick turned to Hoyt. "You've got some explaining to do." Royal slid the car in gear and pulled away from the back of the station just as the firetruck screeched to a stop up front.

At the Reverend Michael Russell's home, the two men were greeted by an irate preacher and a cool Arthur Vance, both seated at the kitchen table.

"Why are these ruffians being brought here?" Russell demanded.

Vance leaned back in a kitchen chair and regarded the men before him in silence. Hoyt and Dan were surly and appeared even shabbier next to Vance's subdued poise. Hoyt rubbed his bruised jaw while Dan stared down at his shuffling feet.

Vance looked them up and down, and the longer he waited to speak, the more the two men fidgeted.

"Well?" Russell asked Vance.

Vance barely glanced at the preacher. Instead, he gently knocked some tobacco from the bowl of his pipe into an ashtray in the center of the table. He pulled the stem from the pipe and began to carefully clean it with a pipe cleaner. The clock ticked as Russell fumed and Dan fidgeted while Hoyt's face took on crimson hue. Royal and Hick observed Vance's tactics with growing admiration. Finally Hoyt leaned forward, placing his knuckles on the table. "I don't know who you think you are, but you can't keep us here."

"Can't I?" Vance asked in a calm voice not looking up from his pipe.

Hoyt's face took on a crimson hue, and he pounded the kitchen table. "Do you know who my cousin is?"

"Why don't you tell me about your cousin," Vance

replied calmly, setting down the pipe stem and scraping the caked tobacco from the pipe bowl with a metal tool. Barely glancing up, he said, "Feel free to have a seat, gentlemen."

Hoyt and Dan looked at one another and then back at Vance. They shifted their feet and remained standing.

Arthur finally looked up at them fully with a cold, calculated gaze. "Sit," he repeated, more firmly, removing his glasses and cleaning them with his handkerchief.

The two men sat and waited. Vance pulled a packet of tobacco from his inside coat pocket. He methodically inspected the pipe and then filled the bowl, tamping the tobacco. Biting the pipe between his teeth, he took a match and lit it, puffing in short bursts until the tobacco glowed and aromatic smoke filled the room. He leaned back in his chair, crossed his legs, hand on the bowl of the pipe, and studied the two men before him.

He said nothing and seemed to be lost in his own thoughts as he enjoyed his smoke.

After several minutes, Hoyt rose. "I'm not going to sit here for this."

Hick gripped Hoyt's shoulder and shoved him back into the chair.

Hoyt narrowed his eyes and studied Vance. "Who are you?"

"I am one who has the power to put you away for a very, very long time. Unless …"

"Unless what?"

Vance smiled and leaned forward. "I'd like you to entertain me."

Hoyt frowned. "What the hell are you talking about?"

"I'd like to hear a story," Vance said. "A family story."

25

Tuesday, July 20, 1954

"And that's nail number three in the fat bastard's coffin," Carol said, stubbing a cigarette out in an ashtray on the back porch. Ice clinked in her glass as she took a long drink.

Hick stared across the street at darkened, sleepy houses. The nighttime air smelled of humidity, and heat lightning flickered in the distance. The town of Broken Creek was quiet after the earlier excitement of a fire at the police station. Doors were locked and curtains drawn as if the houses themselves had closed their eyes to the town's troubles.

Lost in thought, Hick was startled from his reverie.

"You tired, Hillbilly? You're awful quiet." Hick nodded and she continued. "If half of what Royal says about Brewster is true, he's a real piece of work. To stand there and publicly congratulate himself on saving Thad and Enos Burton by saying he hid them away in the holding cells of the courthouse to protect them from the town's understandable and righteous anger. To twist what he ordered done to make himself look good ..." She shook her head and repeated the part of Brewster's speech Royal had memorized, saying in a mock, male voice, "'It is a mercy I had the foresight to keep the suspects safe. We are not a town of vigilantes. We are better than what happened here tonight. I am thankful that when Senator Richardson comes tomorrow, he will not be greeted by the news that we took the law into our own hands.'" She lit another cigarette and threw the lighter on a crate beside the wall. "He thinks we're dead and is probably congratulating himself as we speak."

Royal reported that the evidence room was reduced to charred remains. Anything or anyone in that room was forever gone and Sheriff Earl Brewster made a great show of being devastated by the loss. The fire was hot enough that there could be no inspection of the scene for several days and as Brewster would be the inspector, no one would have ever learned of Hick's and Carol's demise had they been inside. They would have seemingly disappeared and regardless of the weight of suspicion on Brewster, no amount of investigation by Adam or Royal or even Arthur Vance would have ever uncovered the truth.

Unfortunately, much of the evidence that could have been used against Brewster had also gone up in flames. In spite of this, Arthur Vance was unconcerned. While Brewster might be able to shake off the accusations of kidnapping by Hick and Carol, by saying they were interfering with an investigation and had to be held for safekeeping, it would be harder to defend himself against the testimony of the Reverend Russell, Royal Adkins, and Grover Sutton. This evidence coupled with what he had wrenched from Hoyt and Dan would be more than enough to make a solid case against Sheriff Earl Brewster.

Arthur Vance was heavy on Hick's mind when he felt Carol touch his arm and ask, "Is something wrong?"

Hick was uneasy, though he couldn't say why. He turned to Carol. "Your uncle," he said, with a nod toward the house. "He's—"

"He's a relentless son of a bitch," she interrupted. "And he's damned good at what he does."

"I can't help but feel ..." Hick began.

Carol rolled her eyes. "Please don't tell me you feel sorry for those two. Don't forget, they thought we were inside that police station. They meant to burn us alive."

"No, I don't feel sorry for them at all," Hick said. "Hoyt Smith is a habitual lawbreaker and the sooner he's put away the better for everyone in Broken Creek."

"Then what?" "Carol asked.

Hick shook his head. "I don't know," he said. "I just never knew you could break a man like that. I never realized how effective silence, time, and cold, hard questioning could be."

Arthur Vance's slow, methodical questioning of Hoyt and Dan was bone chilling. The man never once raised his voice. He had the self-assurance and disregard of the powerful. The room in which they sat was stifling hot and, yet, Vance seemed unaffected by the heat. Hick had felt the sweat roll down his spine as he stood behind Hoyt. The room was so close and with Vance's pipe smoke, it was hard to breathe. Hoyt and Dan were forced to wipe their brows with their handkerchiefs over and over again to keep the stinging sweat from their eyes while their shirts grew dark in the armpits.

Not so Arthur Vance. He remained cool and deliberate, as if the very blood in his veins was chilled. No sweat beaded on his forehead, he was seemingly unbothered by the sweltering heat. The prisoners were not offered food or water. No bathroom breaks were allowed and, as the air grew thicker, Hoyt and Dan grew fidgety. As time passed, the prisoners became desperate, their eyes wild like those of trapped animals. Vance had asked Hoyt to "entertain" him and, to Hick, it did seem the agent was enjoying himself. It was now close to two in the morning. The questioning had lasted hours and there was a calculated cruelness in it that caused first Dan and then Hoyt to tell Vance everything he wanted to know.

Carol looked into Hick's face and he saw understanding register in her eyes. "It's just the way it's done. You make your suspect see that they're isolated, that they have no recourse, nowhere to go. Convince them that they're powerless and their only escape is to cooperate." Carol shrugged. "It works."

"It sure does. Hoyt Smith may have been saved from federal prison by his cousin, Earl, seven years back, but no one can save him now."

"And he spilled enough information to find who really ran over that man, and to put your Brewster away for life as well," Carol agreed. "At least you know what became of the witness."

Hoyt Smith, like so many others had a debt to pay to Earl Brewster ... that being his avoidance of prison for breaking into the Cherokee Crossing Post Office. He had been Brewster's lackey for years, and under the intense scrutiny of Arthur Vance, had divulged the fact that, at the sheriff's bidding, he had picked up Pack Barnes and, saying he was hallucinating, had him locked away in the State Mental Hospital in Little Rock.

"When Royal returns after speaking with Pack I'm sure we'll know who ran down that vagrant. The town of Broken Creek, Arkansas will be out from under Brewster's yoke, Thad will be free, and the case will be closed. And, yet, it's clear Vance doesn't give a damn about any of this. What about Richardson?" Hick asked. "What's the plan?"

"I don't know any particulars. I only know Uncle Arthur is trying to make a name for the Civil Rights Section of the Justice Department. As he said, he'd like it to be recognized as its own Division and I guarantee you that cuffing some two-bit sheriff and his kin won't do it." She hesitated, seemingly realizing what she was implying, and then continued, "If Richardson and Brewster have made some sort of agreement, if promises of promotion or financial compensation have been made, and most importantly, if they have conspired to suppress the colored vote like my uncle suspects, this will be huge. It will show that while everyone has been distracted by McCarthy's witch hunt, real evil has gone unpunished."

"How does he think he can do this?"

"My guess is Brewster needs to be backed into a corner. He needs to know that we're on to him and that he's in deep. Once that's established, Uncle Arthur can offer him some kind of deal. He doesn't seem like the type to take the fall for someone else."

Hick laughed. "No one would accuse Brewster of loyalty or integrity," he agreed. "So what are we supposed to do? Arrest him?"

Arthur Vance entered the room, smoking his pipe. "I see you're still up."

"Sleep's hard to come by with so much going on," Hick said. "Besides, I hardly feel welcome here in the good reverend's house."

Nodding, Vance slowly looked Hick up and down. "Tell me," he said. "Why are you here? You're a sheriff from another town, with no stake at all in the outcome of these events."

"The priest at the Catholic Church here in town called me. His secretary is Thad's big sister."

Vance shook his head. "That doesn't explain why you're here. What exactly do you expect to gain from this?"

"I don't expect to gain anything," Hick said with a frown.

"Then why risk your life? You could have easily been killed at that jailhouse."

"I know that."

"Then why?"

Hick's heart began to thud against his ribcage as his frustration rose. What was Vance trying to prove? He looked the older man in the eye and said, coldly, "Sometimes you just do things because they're right. In the war I did what I was told. I sat by and watched one too many wrongs because I was afraid to speak up. And I did things I shouldn't have done. Yet I survived. I made it home. Now, I don't intend to live the rest of my life sitting by and keeping my mouth shut. I did that before, and I'll be damned if I ever do it again."

Vance's face barely changed, though his brows rose slightly. "Good. As long as we're all on the same page." He turned and went back into the house. "Step inside," he called behind him. "We have some things to discuss."

Hick hadn't realized his fist was clenched until he felt Carol's hand cover it. He turned to her and she shook her head slightly. "Here," she said, fishing out an ice cube from her glass and wrapping it in her handkerchief. "Your eye is swelling." She paused. "You know he's only doing his job."

Hick let a ragged breath escape and then pursed his lips. He recognized that Vance was very good at what he did, but he didn't have to like him. Forcing a small smile at Carol, he followed Vance into the kitchen.

Arthur was already seated at the table, the ever present pipe was in two pieces and he was using a pipe cleaner on the stem again. He barely glanced up as Hick and Carol sat across from him.

"I understand there's to be a hearing tomorrow," Vance said not looking up.

"The judge and the prosecutor are back in town from their fishing trip," Carol said.

"And these two, the judge and prosecutor," Vance said. "Do we think they're in on this?"

Carol shook her head. "There's no way to prove what they do or don't know. They were gone when the crime took place and have not been briefed on any of the particulars to my knowledge. As far as they're both concerned, all these proceedings are supposed to be nothing more than a hearing for Thad to plead guilty and sentence him."

"I see," Vance replied, filling his bowl with tobacco. "And the courthouse, Thad and his father will be safe there tonight?"

Hick nodded. "Brewster has more to gain in keeping them safe than in allowing harm to come to them. He thinks this is as good as done. In his mind, tomorrow night he'll be at that rally and the whole town will be up in arms over desegregation and practically begging to give Richardson their vote or even their money if he asks."

Vance glanced at his watch. "The hearing commences in a little more than six hours. Our advantage over Brewster is the element of surprise. He doesn't suspect you're still alive or that the federal government has any knowledge of what is happening." He puffed on his pipe until the tobacco burned red. "I understand the State Police will be here?"

"According to Royal, Brewster called then in to protect public property," Hick said. "He pointed to the burning of the police station as cause enough for their help. He doesn't want anyone in the courtroom for this hearing but the judge. Not Thad's mama or sister, and especially not Father Grant. He wants a quick guilty plea and a fast hearing."

Vance leaned back and puffed his pipe. His glance went from Hick to Carol. "I need you two there. Your presence in the courtroom will be unexpected and will throw Brewster off his game. We need him uncomfortable and unsteady so he'll be more inclined to tell us what we want to know."

"What about you?" Hick asked.

Vance smiled. "Oh, I'll be there. I believe I'll pay an early morning call on the judge and give him an escort to the courthouse." He glanced at his watch. "Brewster's deputy ought to be in Little Rock by now to question this Pack Barnes character. Hopefully he really does know something about the hit and run."

"If he doesn't?" Hick asked.

"I believe by the time I arrive with the Right Honorable Judge, he will be less inclined to indict Thaddeus Burton, whether he is Brewster's blood kin or not. I don't foresee any charges being filed." He leaned back and puffed his pipe. "Just for fun, let's suppose a worst case scenario and pretend that this judge decides to charge the young man." He smiled an affectionate smile at his niece. "With the excellent legal advice he has, I am confident we would obtain a good defense and a favorable verdict." Carol smiled at the rare, but genuine compliment from her uncle.

Vance leaned forward and folded his hands. "The key is to make Brewster sweat. I want you to simply sit in the courtroom. Don't say a word, don't do anything. Just sit there. Your return from the dead and appearance in a supposedly sealed courtroom will shatter his smug control. I'd like to chip away at that one piece at a time. First, you enter the courtroom, in spite of the state police barrier, next I'll arrive with the judge. And I can promise you this, that judge will not be in an amiable mood when we arrive. It will not be long before it is clear to Brewster that we have a very good understanding of what he has been doing here in this town. By the time I am finished chatting with him, he will be begging to tell us anything we want to know about Senator Richardson."

"That's all well and good," Carol said, "but how do you propose we get in?" Vance's eyes glanced up toward the second story of the house. "We have a preacher at our disposal. I suggest we use him. Carol, can you ask him to join us?"

Carol left and moments later the Reverend Michael Russell appeared. He was livid as he entered the kitchen. "It's three in the morning," he said in disbelief. "What is the meaning of this? I have allowed you to imprison those two miscreants in my cellar and have given you full run of the house. Now what do you want?"

"We will be requiring your services tomorrow at the courthouse," Arthur Vance said.

"My services?"

"Yes, your status as clergy is something we can use to our advantage."

Russell's eyes widened. "How dare you strong arm me into using my position for your ... your schemes," he sputtered.

Arthur Vance slowly and deliberately removed his glasses and cleaned them with his handkerchief. He put them back on, cocked his head, and regarded the angry preacher. "Your involvement in Sheriff Brewster's scheme dictates your cooperation in ours. Unless, of course, you would prefer ..." he let his voice trail away and didn't finish the sentence.

Russell narrowed his eyes. "Is this a threat?"

"No," Vance replied mildly. "It is a promise. Conspiracy to falsely imprison an innocent person is something we at the Justice Department take very seriously."

Michael Russell's face paled. His mouth opened and closed. Then opened and closed again. Finally, he sighed heavily and looked into Arthur Vance's face. "What is it you would have me do?"

26

Wednesday, July 20, 1954

Thunder rumbled off in the distance. The sunrise was obscured by gray clouds and the air had an electric, stormy smell. Hick stood at the kitchen window, sipping a cup of coffee, and staring bleary-eyed off into the distance. He had tried to sleep on the couch, but sleep would not come. The moment his eyes closed, he would jerk awake, his mind flooded with thoughts and anxiety. He finally got up at 5:00 a.m. and made a pot of coffee.

He glanced at Carol, curled up in an arm chair, sound asleep and smiled to himself, amazed anyone could sleep in such a cramped position. She was unlike any woman he had ever met, nothing like the girls at home. Decidedly masculine, she cursed, smoked, and stated her opinion without hesitation. There was nothing coy or shy about her.

"So how long have you been married?" she had asked him in the early morning hours as they sat talking quietly on the back porch.

"Six years this month," he said.

"High school sweetheart?"

"Girl next door."

Carol had smiled. "Love is still alive," she said, her eyes turning from him to the darkness outside. "Good to know."

Finishing the coffee and placing the cup in the sink, his thoughts drifted to Cherokee Crossing and he wondered if Maggie was still at Pam's or if she had gone back home. Was she sleeping? Since returning from the war, Hick never slept more than a few hours at a stretch, but he noticed that Maggie had begun to sleep less and less. Her pregnancy had caused her ankles to swell into her calves and she was often up at night walking the floors because of muscle cramps. He wondered if she was awake now and felt an overwhelming desire to be at home. This was taking too long. He needed to be with her. He needed to touch her, to kiss her, to smell her hair tangled in his fingertips. He needed the boys and home and—

"What time is it?" Carol called sleepily from across the room.

"It's early," he answered. "Go back to sleep."

She stretched out like a cat, and then walked toward him rubbing her eyes. "Cigarette?"

"You owe me a pack," he said handing her the cigarettes and the lighter. She cupped her hand over the flame, inhaling deeply. "Holy Christ, it's humid down here," she said, handing him back the lighter.

"It's fixin' to storm."

She ran her hand over her face and yawned. "Everything is damp and clammy. How can you stand it?"

"You just get used to it I guess," he said, with a shrug.

She reached into the cabinet and grabbed a coffee cup, then filled it from the pot on the stove. She took a sip. "You think the storm will hold up until 9:00?"

"I don't know. Why?"

A mischievous smile glimmered in her eyes. "I'd like to look nice for my wedding."

∾

The Reverend Michael Russell pulled his car into the parking spot marked "Clergy" at the county courthouse. The wind had picked up and low, gray clouds scudded across the sky. Perhaps it was the threat of rain or the earliness of the hour, but contrary to what Sheriff Earl Brewster had predicted, there was no one outside the courthouse. No demonstrations, no angry citizens, no one besides two bored state policemen flanking the doorway.

Hick and Carol followed Russell up the stairs and to the door. The reverend reached to open it when the officer to the right said, "Sorry, sir. No one is allowed inside this morning."

Russell feigned surprise. "What do you mean?"

"There's a hearing going on of a delicate nature. You know, the colored boy?" He paused, then continued, "The sheriff requested we keep the crowds away."

Michael Russell glared at the young trooper. "To what crowds are you referring?" he asked with a sweep of his arm.

The young man blushed. "If you ask me it's a bunch of

horse crap about nothing. Sheriff says the town is agitated because of the nature of the crime, that being the assault of a white man by this colored boy. Says folks were so riled they burnt the police station to the ground." He glanced around and said, "More than likely some electrical short burnt down that old building." He rolled his eyes. "Ain't one 'agitated' person even looked our way all morning."

The reverend shook his head and pointed at Hick and Carol. "I am the Reverend Michael Russell and you see these two people? They are supposed to be married today, this morning, at my residence. This forgetful young man did not pick up the marriage license. Are they supposed to postpone their wedding due to this imagined hoopla that is supposed to be taking place?"

The trooper shifted his feet and looked to his partner.

"Can't they wait a while?" the other man said. "It's a hearing and once the judge gets here it won't take but a minute."

"We need to catch a train," Hick said.

The two state troopers exchanged glances.

"The licensing office is on the second floor," the reverend explained. "We won't be anywhere near the courtrooms."

Hick noticed Carol's hand growing moist as it rested within his. If this didn't work, there was no Plan B to get inside.

Suddenly, Carol began to sniffle and then to cry. She looked up at the State Trooper. "Look at him! Getting into a fight the night before our wedding. He can't do nothing right. And there's nothing to be done. I can't wait another minute for this wedding." Turning her eyes up to Hick, she added, "We can't wait." Placing her hand over her abdomen, she said in a teary voice "I'll be ruined."

The State Troopers looked at each other and then one nodded. "I understand, Miss." He patted her shoulder. "Everyone makes mistakes." He turned to Hick with a look of disdain. "Go ahead and get the license and then hurry on, get out, and catch your train. Earl Brewster ain't near as important as he thinks he is, but I'd just as soon not have to listen to him complain we didn't do our job."

Carol rested her hand on the trooper's arm. "Thank you, sir," she said, sniffling. "God bless you."

Michael Russell, Hick, and Carol passed the troopers and entered into the courthouse. Once inside, Hick gave Carol an appreciative glance. "Hell, if this attorney thing doesn't work out, you ought to go to Hollywood."

She looked determined. "It's going to work and today's the start of a whole new world for me." She put her hand in the crook of his arm. "Shall we, my dear?"

Hick placed a hand over hers. "Let's get this son of a bitch."

The courthouse was dark and cool, the stone and marble seemed to absorb the sweltering humidity of the impending storm. Carol's pumps clattered on the gleaming, white floor as they made their way across the large foyer and straight to the courtroom. They pushed open the swinging door and sat in a row of seats toward the front.

Royal was the only person inside. "What are ya'll doing here?"

"Vance is coming in with the judge," Hick explained.

"Brewster's day is about to get a mite uncomfortable. Where is he?"

"He's back in the holding cell coaching Thad what to say," Royal said. "To sweeten the deal, he told Enos he'd let him off with just a fine if he makes sure Thad does as he's told."

Carol snorted. "He's a real peach."

"And right now he's happy as a pig in mud," Royal added. "He hasn't called me Dumbass even once today. Although, it's still early."

"Well, his happiness will be short-lived," Hick said with satisfaction. "You talk to Pack?"

Royal shook his head. "I couldn't."

"What do you mean?" Hick asked in surprise. "Why?"

"I went to the hospital to see him, but he was sedated. He's restrained because he's seeing things. He's in the middle of the DTs and they said he's critical. He's in danger of seizures or hurting himself so they had to drug him." Royal sighed. "We'll be able to talk to him in a day or two, but not today. It could be Uncle Earl done something nice for someone by accident. Pack ain't had a drink in over three days and I reckon by the time they're through with him at the hospital, he'll be shed of his drinking problem."

"It doesn't matter," Hick said. "As long as we nab Brewster, the real culprit won't be far behind."

"Speaking of Brewster," Royal said. "I best get back to the holding area to check in."

Adkins left, and Hick, Carol, and Reverend Russell sat in the middle of the silent courtroom and waited, the only sounds the rhythmic ticking from a large clock on the wall and the thunder rolling outside.

At nine o'clock, the door to the courtroom opened and Earl Brewster entered with Thad and Enos Burton. He paused when he saw Hick and Carol in the courtroom and his face flushed. Narrowing his eyes, he muttered under his breath, and led his prisoners to a table in the front of the courtroom to wait for the judge. Brewster sat beside Thad and Royal flanked Enos on the other end of the table. Hick noticed Brewster was fidgety. He tapped a pencil, looked at the clock, and shuffled his feet.

Enos Burton did not turn or acknowledge Hick's presence. His expression when he entered the room was stoic and his body was tense. Hick could see the taut muscles in his neck and noticed his shoulders trembling. Hick thought of his boys, safe at home, and pity threatened to overwhelm him. How must Enos feel knowing his son is in trouble and that he is powerless to help him? How does a man get over that?

Hick recalled the fury in Adam's eyes as he saw Benji's bruised face. Even Willie Taylor's heartbreak seemed poignant to Hick as he considered Hap spending all those years in prison for a crime he didn't commit. And he thought of the Reverend Michael Russell, seated beside him, and the terrible injustice he had allowed to happen in order to save his own son. To what lengths would he go to keep his own children safe?

Suddenly, Hick's heart seized up as a thought occurred to him. A realization so clear, that he was stunned. It was so obvious, he couldn't believe he'd just thought of it. Thunder crashed nearby and Hick realized he had stopped breathing. He caught his breath and turned to Carol. "I know who did it," he said under his breath.

"What?" she whispered. "What are you talking about?"

"I know who ran over the vagrant." He rose quickly, his chair scraping loudly across the floor. Sheriff Brewster jumped in his seat, then turned around. "I'll be back," Hick whispered.

She reached for him. "But Uncle Arthur said—"

"I know," Hick answered. "But I need to see someone now."

He strode through the courtroom toward the door when it burst open, admitting a soaking wet Arthur Vance and Judge Henry Watson. Arthur was surprised to see Hick moving toward the door. "Where are you going?"

"The hit and run. I know who did it," Hick said quietly so Brewster couldn't hear.

Arthur looked at him closely. "You sure?"

Hick nodded.

"Then bring him here."

"I aim to."

The judge didn't pause, but had continued his march to the front of courtroom. Hick heard him say, "Earl, this is highly irregular. Highly irregular." Judge Watson removed his overcoat and shook the rain from it. "I had to come out in this infernal storm and then I get a visit first thing of a morning from the Justice Department—"

"The Justice Department?" Brewster choked.

Hick stopped in the doorway and turned to see Earl Brewster place his hands on the table in front of him for support. Brewster glanced at Hick, stunned surprise clearly written on his face. His face was pale and his eyes frightened. He turned to Judge Watson. "I'm not sure what this is all about."

"Neither am I," Judge Watson replied. "But you'd better have a damned good case against this kid or I'm not charging him. Got it?"

"Case?" Brewster said. "But he's planning on pleading guil—"

Brewster got no further as Ida Burton brushed past Hick into the courtroom. "He will not plead guilty," Ida Burton declared, her voice ringing in the mostly empty room. "My child will not plead guilty for a crime he could not have committed. I will not stand by and let this happen."

Enos rose and faced his wife. "Ida, I done told—"

Brewster stared. "How did you get in here?"

Ida Burton's chin raised and she looked at Earl Brewster as if he were vermin. "I came in through the front door."

Hick noticed a small smile on the face of Royal Adkins and understood that when he walked outside the two state policemen would be gone, officially excused from their duty by Deputy Adkins.

The judge was behind his desk, flipping papers and pushing things around. "Where the hell is my gavel?" he said in an angry voice.

With one last glance at the chaos inside the courtroom, Hick walked into the storm.

27

Wednesday, July 20, 1954

Ike Davis stood in front of the Broken Creek High School staring silently at the building. Hick came up behind him and said, "Reminds me of the old high school in Cherokee Crossing. It's closed now, but my daddy was the principal for years."

Ike glanced at Hick. "I remember when it closed and the kids got transferred to Pocahontas. Upheaval is never good."

"I don't know about that," Hick said. "The kids in Cherokee Crossing got to mingle with other kids, different ones, and they got along and learned from each other. The school closing was hard for the town at first, but change always is."

"Maybe," Davis said with a shrug. "I heard you went back home to Cherokee Crossing yesterday."

"No. I decided to stay in town for Thad's hearing."

Davis winced a little and turned back to the school. "I guess he's probably been sentenced by now."

"I wouldn't count on it," Hick answered. "Thad's mama is evidently putting a stop to that scheme."

"Oh?" Davis said with a hint of surprise. "So Thad will plead not guilty after all."

"I think the judge will dismiss the case. Not enough evidence."

"I see," was all Davis said, but Hick noticed a small sigh escape him. His shoulders relaxed and Hick couldn't help but think that it was relief that covered the school board president's face.

"Interesting that there's not even enough evidence to charge Thad and yet Mr. Enos Burton was hell bent on him pleading guilty," Hick said in a quiet voice, looking at the school and not Ike Davis. "It's funny the things fathers do to protect their sons."

Ike Davis's eyes closed. He stood motionless a moment and then said, "I suppose it is." He turned to Hick. "You got kids?"

"Two boys and one on the way."

"You know, as a father you want what's best for your kids. You work your ass off to give them a good life and they turn out decent. And then in an instant, in one goddamned instant, everything is changed and nothing will ever be the same."

An overwhelming sadness filled Hick and he cleared his throat. "I reckon as a father I can teach my boys one of two things. I can teach them to walk away from their problems and let someone else deal with them, or I can teach them to be men and to face the consequences of what they've done." Hick paused. "Why are you here, Mr. Davis?"

Ike's gaze traveled to the school. "I've been bringing my

boy here of a morning because his car's been broke down."
He looked into Hick's face and added, with meaning, "It's
been broke down for over two weeks."

"I see."

Ike's face crumpled and his lips trembled. His eyes glis-
tened with tears and he turned a knowing gaze on Hick.
"He's seventeen years old." There was a wild, helpless plea in
his eyes. "Will they try him as an adult?"

Hick shrugged. "I don't know. But if he doesn't turn himself in he'll spend his whole life wishing he'd done the right
thing when he had the chance. I'm talking from experience.
There are some mistakes we make that can't ever be made
right, but you're one of the lucky ones. You can, at least, not
make things worse for your boy. He killed a man and he will
live with that forever. Don't let him live with the guilt of
running away from it and having to hide it for the rest of his
life. Don't let him live with the guilt of having another boy
accused for something he didn't do."

Ike ran his hand over his eyes. "When Brewster showed up
at the house in the middle of the night with Billy all bandaged
up and bleeding, he made it seem so simple. Keep my mouth
shut, let him take care of things." He shook his head. "But
it's not simple, is it? It's not easy to sit by and watch another
man's son take responsibility for what your son did."

At that moment the door to the school opened and Billy
Davis came walking down the steps, wearing his letterman's
jacket. He seemed surprised to see Hick, but turned to his
father. The boy's face was strained, there were dark circles
beneath his eyes and tears pooled in them. "Dad?"

Ike Davis put his hand on his son's shoulder and looked into his face. "What is it, son?"

Billy shook his head. "I can't do this. If we hurry we can stop the hearing."

Ike Davis covered his face with his hand and began to sob, but when he removed the hand, his face shone with a mixture of misery and pride. "Yes, Billy. You're right." He turned to Hick. "If you'll excuse us."

Hick nodded and watched father and son walk toward Ike's car. Billy paused beside it and winced as he removed the letterman jacket. Beneath it, his shoulder and arm were bandaged tight. He looked at the jacket for a moment, the last vestige of his childhood, and then climbed beside his father. Hick stood there in the parking lot until the car was out of sight.

∾

When he returned to the courthouse, Hick was surprised to find Wayne Murphy and another man outside with a group of photographers. Murphy grabbed his arm and said, "I came here for the rally but I hear they found the guy that killed the vagrant. It wasn't the little colored boy after all."

"No," Hick said. "It wasn't."

"Son of the president of the school board. That'll go over the fold for sure."

Hick frowned. "Don't you ever get tired of making a living off of everyone else's misery?"

Wayne shrugged. "There's worse ways to make a living.

And that vagrant, I understand he's been identified?"

Hick nodded. "His name is Claud Hayes and he's from Carroll County. I reckon by now Deputy Adkins has contacted the family."

Murphy was writing. "Hayes. Wonder what he was doing in this neck of the woods?"

"Probably looking for work," Hick said. "I'm sure his wife can tell us something once she knows."

Murphy was writing and looked up. "You got anything else for me?"

"Not yet," Hick said. "But stick around. There could be something big happening here tonight. Bigger than the rally."

"Thanks for the tip," Wayne said, tapping his pencil on his notebook. "I'm not going anywhere."

"Well I am," Hick said. "I'm getting home to my family as soon as I say my good-byes. Good luck tonight. I hope you find something worth printing."

"I plan on it," Murphy answered, smiling wide enough to show off his gold tooth.

Hick walked into the courthouse and was greeted by a smiling Carol Quinn and a satisfied-looking Arthur Vance.

"It was the school board president's kid all along," Carol said with a shake of her head. "How'd you figure it out?"

"I just started thinking about what people will do for their kids, and it all made sense. It was the only explanation for the sudden change in Davis's stance on desegregation."

"A dislocated shoulder," Carol said as they walked into the courtroom where Ike and Billy Davis were in close conversation with Judge Watson and Royal Adkins. "An injury that was easy to hide."

"What will happen to him?" Hick asked.

"If Ike Davis will agree to testify against Sheriff Brewster," Carol said, "they'll charge his son as a minor. It won't be easy on him, but it could be a whole lot worse."

Hick glanced around the courtroom. "Where's Thad?"

"All charges were dropped in light of Davis' confession. The whole family marched out the front door, past that damned throng of reporters, and are probably at home celebrating right now."

Hick nodded as an immense swell of satisfaction washed over him. He had played a small role in making sure Thad Burton, an innocent child, had been released. But the satisfaction was bittersweet with the knowledge that Billy Davis, a boy who only wanted to "fit in" would be facing a year or two at the prison camp, and a permanently sullied reputation. Hick knew, better than most, that some mistakes never leave you.

"What did ya'll do with Brewster?" Hick asked.

"He's in the same holding cell where he kept Thad last night," Carol said. "Uncle Arthur told him what we had on him and Brewster sort of crumbled. He started with Sutton and then the kid and by the time he mentioned the name of Hoyt Smith, the fat bastard had to sit down. Can't say I feel sorry for him, though I wish I could." Carol paused and studied Hick for a moment. "Uncle Arthur's pretty impressed with you. Told me it's not easy to find someone with as much integrity and intuition as you seem to have."

They both turned toward Arthur Vance. Word of Billy's arrest had spread and Arthur was observing the crowd forming in front of the courthouse. "He's letting Brewster sweat it out for a bit before questioning him about Senator Richardson," Carol added. "He told him that he needs to think long and hard about how much punishment he's willing to take for someone else. Then, he reminded him of how hard prison is for cops, especially dirty ones. You can bet Brewster is walking the floors right now."

And then Carol jumped as the crack of a gunshot echoed off the stone walls of the courthouse, reverbrating from wall to floor to ceiling. Hick took off running with Carol's heels clacking distantly behind him. Hick ran to the back of the courthouse, toward the holding cells, and almost collided with Royal as he came running from the opposite direction.

"That came from the holding cell," Royal exclaimed.

Hearing footsteps, they rounded the corner and looked into the cell and stopped short. Sheriff Earl Brewster was staring vacantly up at the ceiling, a bullet hole in the middle of his forehead, and a gun on the floor besides him. Hick looked around frantically and saw that the back door of the courthouse was swinging to and fro. He ran to look outside—but no one was there.

Voices shouted, people came running, and chaos ensued as Royal tried to keep the crowd at bay. Dozens of onlookers and journalists crowded into the narrow hallway and Royal pushed them back and began to close a large metal door. Just before it shut, Hick caught the shocked expression on Carol's face and the dark scowl on Arthur Vance's. There would be no information to indict Senator John Wesley Richardson, after all. Royal pushed everyone back and the door closed, leaving the clamor in the lobby of the courthouse. Hick and Royal faced one another, and Hick noticed how old and tired Royal suddenly appeared. Hick drew in a deep breath and exhaled slowly. The two lawmen stood side by side and looked down at Arthur Vance's key witness, dead on the floor, in a pool of blood.

28

It was a stark, meaningless reminder. A life reduced to engraved letters and numbers. Gone But Not Forgotten. Cold stone and loosened dirt, a cipher of numbers 1926 - 1954. He knew granite would never succeed in capturing her ... the laugh he would do anything to produce, the light in dark eyes that once shone so bright, the smile that lightened his darkest mood. The way she moved. The way she touched him. The way a single look could drive him wild. Maggie had been his everything, and now nothing remained but those damned engraved numbers and letters.

Heedless of the stiff burrs digging into his knees, Hick sank to the ground and let the grief engulf him. He embraced the pain, held it so close it seared through his skin, burning and boiling until it seemed his very blood vessels would explode from the heat. Would to God he could weep, tear his hair, rend his garments, anything to release the pressure living within the very marrow of his bones. But his eyes were dry, the grief too intense to be relieved by mere tears. He'd listened, even if at a distance, to the preacher's sermon and to the people console him, and had heard, in their prayers and expressions of sympathy, their unspoken expectations. So no, he would not weep. He would not tear out his hair, wear sackcloth, or rend his clothes. Instead, Hick Blackburn would shoulder his burden and soldier on.

But then, out of his very core, the scream erupted and he was like some wild thing in the throes of a predator's claws. He screamed, again and again and again and collapsed onto the mound of dirt that covered the girl next door.

He would never forget driving home after a long, hard day at the courthouse in Broken Creek. He would never forget standing silently by and listening to the ridiculous notion that Sheriff Earl Brewster had taken his own life. Although Arthur Vance, Royal Adkins, and Hick had all repeatedly and vehemently argued that his death was not suicide, that the gun in the cell appeared to be tossed there, and that it was evident someone had run from the courthouse leaving the back door swinging open and closed in the storm.

But the coroner's mind was made up and nothing more would be done. Donald Brewster did not want an investigation and he refused to budge. He understood that prying into the affairs of Earl Brewster would damage his brother's reputation, not to mention his own, and he was prepared to protect both at all costs. Finally, Arthur Vance concluded that the list of those who would benefit from Earl Brewster's death was too lengthy and that finding the killer would be next to impossible. So Hick headed for the Broken Creek squad car Royal had loaned him for the drive home.

He'd been in a hurry to get back to Maggie and the boys and felt no inclination to argue the point any longer. He was rushing to his car when Carol had called after him.

"Hillbilly!"

He turned and she smiled. "You were going to leave without saying good-bye?"

"I'm kind of anxious to get home."

She nodded. "I remember. The girl next door. You're one of the lucky ones."

He laughed. "Yes, I am."

"I hear Uncle Arthur offered you a job with the Justice Department. Will you take it?"

The idea was exciting, breathtaking even, but he only said, "I don't know. I'll need to talk it over with my wife."

At that moment, the sun was still shining and all things were possible. A new baby on the way. A new job on the horizon. It wasn't until he was almost back to Cherokee Crossing and he spied Adam's squad car speeding, with lights flashing and siren blaring, toward Broken Creek that the horrible feeling grabbed hold.

Adam careened to a stop and ran to Hick's car, his face flushed.

"What is it?" But Hick already knew.

"Maggie. It's Maggie."

Hick couldn't recall the funeral. He had tried in the ensuing days, but it was as if it never really happened. He knew there had been a service at church. There must have been a burial because here he was in front of a damnable piece of granite that bore witness that his heart had been torn from his body and lay somewhere beneath him. His boys and Mourning were with his sister, and Hick couldn't bring himself to sleep in the house. He had stayed at the station and spoken to no one.

He stretched himself over the earth and whispered, "I'm sorry, I'm sorry, I'm sorry," digging his fingers into the sandy dirt and longing to touch her, to feel her breath on his cheek, hear her whisper, "I love you, Hickory." This time he'd say it back. This time he'd find the words.

How long he had lain on the damp ground, he didn't know, but he felt someone else's presence and turned his bleary eyes to see Jake, whose own face was mottled with grief. With great difficulty, Jake knelt beside Hick, his arm on the younger man's shoulder as if willing it to be a conduit for at least some of Hick's pain to transfer to him. Hick had no idea what day it was, how long he had been at the cemetery, or how long Jake had been watching. He only knew that he wanted, more than anything, to be beside his love, where the pain that threatened to tear him apart, could no longer torment him.

"I was gone," Hick finally managed to say in a hoarse, cracked whisper. "I wasn't even there."

"There was nothing you could have done."

"I should have been there."

"To what purpose? To see her die? This is pointless, Hick. You can't punish yourself. Even if you were there, she wouldn't have known. It was a massive stroke. Mourning said she had a headache and went to lie down. She died in her sleep."

"I can't do this," Hick whispered.

"You have to do this. Your boys need you."

Hick closed his eyes and saw the faces of his sons, tear-stained and bewildered.

"When's the last time you slept?" Jake asked.

"I don't know. I can't go back into that house. I can't. She's everywhere."

"Come home with me," Jake said, struggling to his feet and holding out his hand. "Stay with me for a while. That new deputy, Royal, can help Adam. You need some time." Jake squeezed Hick's shoulder. "Please come with me and let me help you."

Hick hesitated. Maggie was here, he didn't want to go.

"Please," Jake said. "She's not here anymore. She never was."

A tear rolled down Hick's face. And then another. He hadn't realized he was crying until the warm splash landed on the dirt. He sat up and the world reeled around him. Unable to recall when he last ate or slept, Hick rose to his feet, and his knees trembled.

Jake took his hand and Hick looked down into his old friend's saddened face. He let Jake, his father's oldest friend and his own trusted confidant, lead him by the hand like he was a little boy. He paused at Jake's car and turned back to the cemetery. Maggie's grave was very near his father's. It read Magdalene Benson Blackburn and Child. A life, two lives really, reduced to meaningless letters and numbers.

Gone But Not Forgotten.

Never forgotten.

Acknowledgments

Thank you to all who have come to know and care about Hick Blackburn and for challenging me with "what's next?" A great deal of thanks is owed to Mr. Bill Hopkins for his advice and insight into the legal system. Thank you to my writer's group: Paula Bircher, Deborah Weltman, and Tom Boyd for your encouragement and for traveling with me on this journey. I am grateful to Bob Dilg and Steve Graham for their criticism and encouragement and to Ronni Graham, Katherine Ising, and Debbie Pilla for your support. Thank you to all who have been with me from the start, urging me on, and inspiring me to not give up. And, lastly, thank you to Kristina Blank Makansi, Donna Essner, and Lisa Miller for your unwavering support and belief in Hick and Cherokee Crossing.

About the Author

Cynthia A. Graham is the winner of several writing awards, including a Gold IPPY, two Midwest Book Awards, and was named a finalist for the Oklahoma Book Award. Her short stories have appeared in both university and national literary publications. She attained a B.A. in English from the Pierre Laclede Honors College at the University of Missouri in St. Louis. Cynthia is a member of the Historical Novel Society, the St. Louis Writers' Guild, the Missouri Writers' Guild, and Sisters in Crime.

CPSIA information can be obtained
at www.ICGtesting.com
Printed in the USA
LVOW03s0347130218
566346LV00001B/1/P